HOT RAGE AND COLD STEEL

Willie and his sidekick were too busy playing around with Jennifer Blake to notice Skye Fargo until he pressed cold steel against Willie's neck. "Stand up slow and easy."

Willie instead lunged forward to get away from the blade, while his partner bolted.

The knife went down. Willie's howl split the night air as his blood sprayed all over the shed. Skye didn't have time to duck the bullet the partner sent at him. He leapt forward to gain ground, hollering loud on the way, as if wounded. But the gunman wasn't taking any chances. He leveled his pistol again, and point-blank pulled the trigger. . . .

The Trailsman was in a one-man war—and no one was taking prisoners. . . .

Ⓞ SIGNET WESTERNS BY JON SHARPE

(0451)

RIDE THE WILD TRAIL

Prices slightly higher in Canada

THE TRAILSMAN 94

DESPERATE DISPATCH

by

Jon Sharpe

A SIGNET BOOK

NEW AMERICAN LIBRARY

A DIVISION OF PENGUIN BOOKS USA INC.

NAL BOOKS ARE AVAILABLE AT QUANTITY DISCOUNTS
WHEN USED TO PROMOTE PRODUCTS OR SERVICES.
FOR INFORMATION PLEASE WRITE TO PREMIUM MARKETING DIVISION,
NEW AMERICAN LIBRARY, 1633 BROADWAY,
NEW YORK, NEW YORK 10019.

The first chapter of this book previously appeared in
The Texas Train, the ninety-third book in this series.

SIGNET TRADEMARK REG. U.S. PAT. OFF. AND FOREIGN COUNTRIES
REGISTERED TRADEMARK—MARCA REGISTRADA
HECHO EN DRESDEN, TN, USA

SIGNET, SIGNET CLASSIC, MENTOR, ONYX, PLUME, MERIDIAN
AND NAL BOOKS are published by New American Library,
a division of Penguin Books USA Inc.,
1633 Broadway, New York, New York 10019

First Printing, October, 1989

1 2 3 4 5 6 7 8 9

PRINTED IN THE UNITED STATES OF AMERICA

The Trailsman

Beginnings . . . they bend the tree and they mark the man. Skye Fargo was born when he was eighteen. Terror was his midwife, vengeance his first cry. Killing spawned Skye Fargo, ruthless, cold-blooded murder. Out of the acrid smoke of gunpowder still hanging in the air, he rose, cried out a promise never forgotten.

The Trailsman, they began to call him, all across the West: searcher, scout, hunter, the man who could see where others only looked, his skills for hire but not his soul, the man who lived each day to the fullest, yet trailed each tomorrow. Skye Fargo, the Trailsman, the seeker who could take the wildness of a land and the wanting of a woman and make them his own.

*Early summer, 1860, in St. Joseph, Missouri,
where the Pony Express has just
begun—and men are already dying
to get the messages . . .*

1

As the shadows lengthened and a bit of welcome evening coolness invaded the stifling and humid afternoon air, the tall man halted his big pinto stallion. Before dismounting, he mopped at his sweaty, dust-streaked brow with the greasy right arm of his buckskin shirt. Instantly he regretted the action. His nose wrinkled in disgust as he shook his shoulder-length black hair. That just meant his nose was assaulted by yet another collection of repulsive odors, mostly stale and all rank.

Broad-shouldered but whipcord-lean, Skye Fargo assured his Ovaro, whose nostrils flared in dismay whenever Fargo got close, that they'd all feel a lot better within the hour. He tied the reins to the hitch rail that stretched in front of a two-story stone building just off the main street of St. Joseph, Missouri.

The gaudy sign over the door said it was the Alhambra Royal Turkish Bathhouse, Strictly Modern in All Respects, Cleansing Waters of Sparkling Purity, Heated by Steam. That was exactly the place the Trailsman desperately needed to visit after a month of persuading a dozen mule-drawn wagons to cross the Great Plains.

The men who owned that shipment had been in a hurry. Up in Blackhawk, a mining camp six hundred miles away in the westernmost mountains of Kansas Territory, the deepening mines had encountered a new kind of ore. Its gold was so bound in with other minerals that the usual ground-shaking stamp mills couldn't extract the precious metal. The way the mine owners explained it, they needed to ship ten tons of their confusing rock to Swansea just as fast as humanly possible, before they went broke.

Swansea was a world-renowned smelting center, with high-powered experts who could find a refining process for that refractory ore. Swansea was also across the ocean, in Wales, but they hadn't expected Fargo to take their shipment that far. Just to Missouri to get it eastbound on the Hannibal & St. Joseph Railroad, fast, and damn the expense.

The Trailsman liked jobs like that, but pushing that hard meant there had hardly been time to eat, let alone pause for anything as frivolous as a real bath. He was sure that even the stinking mules smelled better than he did, since they at least got curried every night.

A reeking puff of dust arose from Fargo's shirt pocket when he patted it, then looked down to be sure he was still carrying the bill of lading from the St. Joe station agent, written confirmation that he had done the job. When he turned that in at the bank, a draft would be waiting, which he could cash. Then he'd have to visit the saloons and whorehouses to find his trail crew and pay them off. He'd probably have to go by the jail and bail a few of them out, too.

Earlier today, the railroad agent had taken half of forever to handle a half-hour job. By the time the consignment got shoveled into a gondola car and the paperwork got filled out, three o'clock had come and gone, so the bank was closed until tomorrow. That may have been just as well. Fargo knew he had no business appearing in public until he had a bath and some clean clothes.

From his saddlebag, he pulled out the paper-wrapped parcel he had just purchased from the pimply-faced clerk who had obviously been more than eager to hurry the reeking Trailsman out of his nice, clean store. But Fargo's money had been good for a new hickory shirt, a stiff pair of Levi's, new balbriggans, and the luxury of clean, dry socks.

When the Trailsman turned and started around the hitch rail, he saw a woman strolling on the boardwalk, swirling a parasol as she came his way. Even though the afternoon was getting on, it was a little early for her kind to be on the street. His mind was still set on a bath, but Fargo didn't mind a momentary distraction to enjoy the scenery.

Her crimson hat, with the shine of satin, had to be the latest style from back East, since it was something Fargo had never seen before. Most ladies' hats these days were small, just covering the crown of the head. Hers was like that, except it had a stiff appendage on the back that went out for a few inches, then dropped for about a foot, thus sheltering a profusion of golden curls that cascaded rearward.

Despite the small size of the crown, her hat sported more feathers than a Cheyenne war bonnet, though hers were egret, not eagle, and were all bunched up and tied together with silk. Expertly applied black kohl made her darting blue eyes look bigger than they were, and she had a sort of wholesome apple-cheeked look, although Fargo knew rouge when he saw it.

He also knew expensive goods when he saw them. Her beribboned saffron taffeta dress boasted a neckline that was far too low for any respectable woman. The swirling parasol kept the potent sunshine off the creamy skin of her well-rounded and prominent breasts, exposed almost down to the nipples. But the parasol didn't do a thing to stop Fargo's eager eyes from savoring the pleasant sight. Not only was it enjoyable to watch her breathe, she sauntered in such a way that her long skirts kept flouncing up to reveal well-turned ankle above her slipperlike shoes.

"At least twenty dollars a night," Fargo muttered as he recalled his mission and began to turn toward the plank door of the Alhambra. He told his rising desire to simmer down, since he wasn't going to have any double eagles to spend on an end-of-the-trail celebration until he got to the bank tomorrow.

"Good afternoon, sir," the woman greeted, her voice low and throaty. "Are you new in town?"

Momentarily nonplussed by her brazenness, Fargo just nodded. He could detect her lilac cologne. Maybe that explained why she was approaching him. She was upwind, and still ten feet away. She just hadn't got close enough to get a whiff of an unwashed trailsman who had maybe two dollars in his pockets.

She stepped closer and got wind of him. He could tell by how she momentarily wrinkled her upturned nose. That should have ended this encounter, but she continued to sashay forward, her eyes scanning him from muck-caked boots to smoke-streaked hat. (The only way you could start a buffalo-chip fire was by fanning furiously, and Fargo's wide-brimmed, beaver-felt hat was generally the most convenient fan.)

"Did you just arrive from California?"

Fargo hadn't noticed before just how long her eyelashes were, but he couldn't miss them now, the way they batted like frolicking butterflies.

"Rocky Mountains," he grunted as he shifted his parcel of new clothes from his right arm to his left, so he'd have an easier time pushing the Alhambra's door open as soon as this high-class harlot gave up on him.

"Oh, really." She brightened. "Would you like to tell me about your journey?" Her neck twisted as she scanned the street, which was pretty much empty. Nobody was within fifty yards on this lazy summer afternoon; even over on the main street, a block away, hardly any traffic disturbed the dust. Her eager gaze returned to the Trailsman. "I have a room nearby where we could talk. You could relax with a drink."

Her sultry tone made it clear that Fargo could expect considerably more than conversation and a shot of whiskey. But this wasn't adding up right. Fargo had been accosted on the streets often, sometimes even in broad daylight. The women who solicited directly were usually missing teeth, overly plump, scar-faced, or just too old to work in the classier parlor houses.

The exquisite creature before Fargo could have been the star attraction at any high-toned bordello this side of San Francisco. Yet she was throwing herself at what had to be the grimiest man in town. Fargo felt leery of any woman who'd even consider bedding him in his current state; it was kind of sickening to think of what else she might have taken in if she was willing to take Fargo now.

"Honey," he explained, "as you've doubtlessly noticed, I need a bath worse that I need anything else right now. So, let me tend to that, and if we run across each other later, we can figure out something then. I'm sure we'd both enjoy it more."

"Oh, I have a brand-new galvanized tub at my place," she chirped. "And I could make sure you got good and clean all over." She regarded him again, as if to make sure he fit a description she was carrying in her pretty little head, before lifting her gloved right hand. "My name is Penelope. You can call me Penny if you'd like. And your name is?"

Fargo doubted like hell that she'd been christened Penelope at her birth about twenty years ago, so he didn't feel any qualms about plucking a name from the air. Besides, he'd prefer that, while he was in town, his name was connected to someone a lot cleaner than he was at the moment. He clasped her right hand with his and left some appalling smudges on her delicate lace-trimmed white cotton glove.

"Jethro." He smiled. "Jethro Hoon." He gazed into her darkening eyes as her face fell. "Know where there's any work to be found hereabouts? I can bust mules, swamp saloons, stoke boilers, shovel stalls, just about any old thing that needs to be done."

Her exasperated sigh interrupted Fargo. To see what would come of it, he didn't finish turning toward the door.

"But, but," she spluttered.

"But what?"

"But you look so much like him."

"Like who?"

"Hasn't anyone ever told you how much you look like Skye Fargo, the Trailsman?"

What the hell was going on here? Penelope looked to be about as short on brains as she was long in other departments, so somebody had put her up to this. For all he knew, there could be an accomplice as well as the offered tub and implied bed waiting for him at Penelope's room. Any other time, it might have been interesting to go find out. But he was tired and dirty, so he stuck with being Jethro.

He shrugged. "Mayhaps. Don't recollect exactly. Anybody ever tell you how much you look like Delilah, honey?"

He had no idea how she responded to that, because he almost jumped to the bathhouse door and got it slammed behind him a moment later. He looked for a bar or chain latch, just to be sure that he and Penelope had parted company, but through the small window he could see her lift her skirts and traipse away.

The pasty-faced clerk stirred himself, yawned, and got to the counter. As hot and muggy as it was in here, it was no wonder the clerk acted slothful. But his surprisingly baritone voice could sure move at a fair clip.

"What will it be, sir? We have authentic Turkish luxury baths, an exact replica of those used by Sultan Yusuf the First at the original Alhambra Castle, which offer the discerning bather a luxurious warm room, an elegant hot room and a palatial steam room, for the ultimate in personal sanitation. Why, it even cleanses the very depths of your pores, so that your skin can breathe. Many people are not aware—and you may be among those unfortunates—that clogged pores often result in neurasthenia, consumption and other pulmonary disorders, neuralgia, dyspepsia, female complaints—"

Fargo interrupted the practiced presentation. "Just a plain old bath in a plain old tub, if you offer such. If not, point me to somewhere that does."

"Why, certainly, sir. Always glad to oblige a customer, we are. But I feel compelled to inform you that we have no 'plain old' tubs. Certainly ours follow the hallowed tradition—none of that newfangled galvanized iron here—but our supremely comfortable individual bathing basins are constructed of none but the stoutest, quarter-sawn white oak from the great hardwood forests of Michigan. Master coopers assemble these—"

"Look," Fargo interjected again. "I just want some hot water to sit in, and some soap."

Before the clerk could much more than get started about how their pure shining-white soap was made of nothing but the exquisitely rendered tallow of fatted Cincinnati hogs and the ashes of select hardwoods, Fargo interrupted again, and this time, even in the dim, shadowy interior, the clerk could see the menace in his eyes.

"Excuse me, sir. A plain bath. That would be ten cents, payable in advance."

Fargo felt heartened that a bath was so reasonable, even in a place this fancy. He began to fish for a dime. The clerk went on.

"Soap, of course, will be an extra nickel. One of our

special soft towels will be an additional five cents." Fargo continued to dig for change as the total mounted: three cents for a washcloth, another five for a back brush, an extra dime for a change of water, which, as filthy as he was, he'd certainly need. Likely he'd be able to sell his first tub as a barrel of ink to a printing shop. But the total was still considerably less than the whole dollar they charged for the full Turkish bath.

He paid. The clerk excused himself and stepped out into the hall, where he hollered to an upstairs helper to get stall number four ready. When the clerk returned, he had the towel, washcloth, soap, and brush.

"It will take a few moments for our staff to draw your bath upstairs, sir," the clerk explained. "If you wish, you may relax on a chair." He gestured toward a row of straight-backed wooden chairs that looked about as comfortable as sitting on a hot stove.

Fargo had the feeling that his buckskins were so stiff that sitting down would be too much work, anyway, so he declined. "This is a pretty fancy place, for no more business than you're getting," he commented.

"Oh, we do all right," the clerk responded. "Sure, we'd get a lot more trade if we were down by the river, where all the teamsters and freighters would come in. But there are already three bathhouses down there. Where we are, we get a better sort of trade, and they're willing to pay better, too. It's hard to get more than a nickel in that part of town."

"But, hell," Fargo protested, "as nearly as I can tell, you've done all of thirty-eight cents so far today. That's no way to stay in business."

"In the evening, when men want to freshen up for a night on the town, it'll pick up plenty. And on Saturdays we're packed from morning till nigh midnight. Get a big wagon train in, and we'll be busy like that on any old day, soon as those cheap bathhouses fill up."

If he had more to say, it wasn't important. Some thumps from upstairs signaled that the Trailsman's long-awaited bath was ready.

Fargo had not stopped at the Alhambra because it was supposed to be so luxurious; he didn't care. It was just that, after racing across town only to arrive at the bank about ten minutes too late, he turned to the closest spot for a bath, and the Alhambra was just down the street.

But the place was pretty nice. The walls of the stall were whitewashed wood, not just canvas like in the cheap places. There were hooks for his clothes, a pewter pitcher for washing his hair, a chair for comfort before and after, and he'd drink a lot of water that wasn't nearly as clean as what was steaming in the tub.

Eagerly, he sat down, tugged off his boots and socks, then laid his new clothes on the chair, atop his Colt and the thin-edged throwing knife he kept strapped to his leg. He left his buckskins on the floor, figuring that any hot soapy water that splashed on them had to represent an improvement. Tomorrow he'd figure out a way to give them a thorough airing.

Fargo had just settled into the tub when a deep voice boomed from the other side of the door.

"Everybody out . . . now!"

"I need ten minutes and a change of water after that," Fargo shouted to the door.

"When I say now, that means now, not sometime next week, asshole."

"When I pay hard cash for a goddamn bath, I figure on getting my money's worth." Things quieted for a moment, so Fargo decided he had made his point. He reached for the pitcher so he could dampen his hair.

The little lull must have been caused by the man outside stepping back so he had enough leverage to kick in the stall door with one tremendous hobnailed thrust.

Crackling wood flew toward the tub as the hinges and latch yielded with mournful screeches.

The surly red-bearded man nearly filled the doorway with his broad shoulders. His tree-limb arms looked strong enough to tote ten-gallon buckets to fill baths, but one hand was empty and the other pointed a six-shot Remington at Fargo's forehead, and its hammer was already back. Just about anything might set the gun off.

"Out," he commanded.

"What's your problem?" Fargo countered as he improved his grip on the pitcher.

The big man's grin displayed several missing teeth. "I'm not the one with the problem. You are. Now get out."

"Mind telling me why?"

"I'm the one with the gun here." But the huge man's voice mellowed a bit. "No harm in telling you, though, I reckon. Mr. Abernathy wants to take a bath downstairs. And when Mr. Josiah Abernathy takes a bath, he don't want nobody to disturb his comfort."

"So?"

"I am his duly hired personal guard, and the easiest way to make sure nobody disturbs him is to clear the place out. An important man like Mr. Abernathy has lots of enemies."

Fargo caught his drift and saw that the man was getting so exasperated that he wasn't holding the pistol quite so straight anymore. But its muzzle still looked ominous, big enough to crawl down, from where Fargo sat. He wasn't ready to act yet.

"Abernathy?" Fargo wondered aloud, his voice skeptical. "Who the hell is Josiah Abernathy?"

He knew damn well who Josiah Abernathy was. Anybody who'd seen a newspaper in the last four or five years had to be aware of Abernathy, a stock speculator of small morals.

The Remington's muzzle wavered some more as its

holder wondered how he could have found someone who had never heard of Josiah Abernathy.

"Josiah Abernathy is about the richest man in the world," Fargo heard. "More to the point, he's my boss, and he wants you somewhere else." The voice was developing an agitated edge.

Fargo nodded agreeably, but used his apparent cooperation as a distraction. It was time to act. Since the pitcher was sitting right before him, between his knees, he couldn't get much leverage. But he could snap his wrists and elbows with enough force to fling a pitcher's worth of hot soapy water forward, into the big man's astonished eyes.

The man's instant reflex was to fire the pistol. In the tiny chamber, the explosion left Fargo's ears ringing. But the goon had stumbled back to avoid the water, and the Remington bullet plowed through the back of the chair and plunked against the back wall, so spent that it didn't even penetrate but dropped to the floor.

Abernathy's bodyguard pawed at his stinging eyes and tried to find Fargo in the haze of powder smoke. The Trailsman heaved another pitcher that way. Still waving the gun, the man lurched forward, only to step atop Fargo's sweat-slicked buckskins.

The waxed plank floor was sopping wet by now, so the buckskins offered about the same footing that a polished ice pond would. Big hobnailed boots slid backward while the huge man tumbled forward, right hand clutching the revolver while he continued to wipe at this face with his ham-sized left.

Aware that he was as safe in the tub as he was anywhere, Fargo remained in place, although he drew his feet up under him so he could spring up fast if necessary.

But first he needed to lean forward. When the flailing gun came near the water, Fargo chopped the massive wrist with his fist. That was only enough to cause a momentary dip, which sent the cylinder into the water for an instant. Then Fargo leaned farther forward, wet soap in hand, and jabbed the bar at his opponent's blinking eyes.

The green orbs started blinking a lot faster after the soap stung their delicate membranes. The man roared. With every bit of control he could muster, he stared at Fargo's rising figure and thumb-cocked the revolver. At point-blank range, he had a dead shot at Fargo's back as the Trailsman rose and turned to step out of the tub.

When the hammer fell, the percussion cap did its job with a small bang. But that was all that happened in the moment before Fargo got settled on the chair with his dry Colt.

The big man jerked his revolver around and took another shot at the grinning Trailsman. This time, not even the percussion cap went off.

"Stay put for a minute," Fargo commanded, enforcing his words with a menacing motion from the Colt. "Seems to me you disturbed my bath. How do you plan to make it up to me?" Fargo slumped, so that he could reach out and take the man's useless revolver away.

It wasn't quite useless, though. Fargo used it to cold-cock the stretched-out hulk. Then he built a gag out of his old socks, which not only stank to high heaven but felt stiff enough to walk all on their own. He sliced up the bodyguard's leather belt and used some of it to manacle those huge hands behind the man's back. The rest went for hobbles.

Fargo wrapped the towel around him before he peeked out into the hallway, Colt in hand. As he suspected, the upstairs attendant was long gone. But the Trailsman figured he could find a bucket and the source of the hot water, and then set up in another stall. He still needed a good bath, and one way or another, he was going to get one.

He did. The ruckus downstairs didn't start until the Trailsman was almost dressed, with just his boots to pull on.

2

After a moment of sober reflection, Fargo realized the noise wasn't coming from downstairs, but from out in the street. He spun and padded past the bath stalls to the front windows. At the edge of the rightmost of the tall, narrow windows he shifted the curtain for a discreet peek.

At least half of St. Joseph had to be milling around outside, hollering and whooping. Then a cannon went off. No one on the street appeared to be bothered by the explosion, though. Instead, men were adding to it by firing their pistols in the air. The coffee-colored surface of the Missouri River was hidden by the bluffs that supported hilly St. Joe. All Fargo could see that way were twin smokestacks poking up above some buildings. The soot-stained stacks were moving slowly, toward town; Fargo recognized them as those of the *Denver*, the steam-powered ferry boat he'd ridden early this morning to cross the river from Elwood, Kansas.

Several low-pitched toots from the boat's whistle were answered by more assorted pistol shots and several shrill blasts from the whistle of a steamed-up locomotive waiting in the yards on the other side of town. The stacks quit moving. Their smoke no longer emerged in chalky puffs, but settled to a steady, if small, black plume.

So the ferry was docking, but that happened a dozen times every day. St. Joe had to be one boring town if that was enough to stir such excitement. Fargo didn't recall any such fanfare when he'd led his Ovaro and the ore wagons off the boat.

The energetic crowd below began to shift out of the center of the street and to jam the sidewalks, as if they were making way for a parade that was coming their way. Perhaps a circus had just arrived in town, but as Fargo strained his eyes for elephants while listening for the first beats of a big bass drum and the unmistakable pitch of a calliope, he found no sign of a circus.

All that came up the street was a skinny kid atop a dun horse, which he was spurring furiously while he applied a quirt to its sweaty flanks, as if he were trying to outrun a rope-minded posse. But he was obviously the hero of this St. Joe celebration, since the crowd was waving and cheering him on. As the rider pounded closer, Fargo got a clearer view of the rigging.

The saddle was much lighter than the general run, and it sprouted leather pouches that flanked the rider's thighs, fore and aft, on both sides. Those pouches, about a foot deep, were part of the *mochila*, which was thrown over the saddle seat and secured by holes that let the horn and cantle stick through. This particular *mochila* had been in San Francisco—about two thousand miles away—just eleven days ago. The Pony Express had just crossed the continent again with mail from the West Coast; this was the final leg.

All eyes turned up the street as the rider pounded past. Stirring up a house-sized cloud of dust, he reined his horse to a halt, vaulted from his saddle, and tossed the *mochila* to the waiting agent before the door of a substantial two-story brick building that served as both the local office and the national headquarters of the largest freighting company in the world: Russell, Majors & Waddell, which also owned the Pony Express.

What the Trailsman knew about the Pony Express was

mostly hearsay from campfire tales and livery-stable gossip. What he knew directly was that he had seen several of its riders dash past his recent caravan along the Overland Trail.

The service had just started last April. It had been an audacious notion, that anybody could haul messages that fast for that far, but from all accounts, it was working. No matter where you went, people were excited about the Pony Express. Since the idea had been hatched in St. Joe, and since the town was one end of the famous connection, that would easily explain why there was so much hoorah here about some kid galloping down the street.

Fargo knew what would happen once the *mochila* got into the office. Its four pouches would be opened and the dispatches inside would be sorted; those that went to St. Joe or nearby would stay, while the others would be sent over to the railroad depot and put aboard the waiting train's express car.

Fargo was about to step back from the window when he saw that two men right below him had also gotten bored. Looking furtive, they were sidling toward the door of the Alhambra. From directly above, Fargo couldn't get a good look at them, but he got the impression that they weren't honest customers. Granted, they both could use baths, judging by how grimy their hands looked. But both were wearing frayed frock coats on a sultry day when wearing any kind of a coat was worse than a burden. One had both hands atop low-hung pistols, while the other kept his left on the pistol while he used his right to fiddle with the door latch, as if he were trying to be sneaky about opening it and stepping inside.

Fargo whirled and raced to the back end of the upper floor of the bathhouse. He paused at the landing to make sure nobody was coming up the stairs, and then, with his revolver before him, he tiptoed down the steps. At the bottom was a closed door directly before him, which likely led to a supply closet. An open door to the left led to the lobby.

He removed his hat and led with that, holding it by the brim. But there weren't any shots, and all Fargo could hear was some shuffling, so he peeked out, just in time to see the two men vanish in a cloud over by the far wall.

No magician was at hand. The desk clerk wouldn't be able to explain this trick, since he was slumped facedown on the counter, blood slowly oozing out of a nasty gash on his forehead. Once the cloud dissipated a bit, Fargo saw a metal door with a tight seal. The portal must lead into the steam room, and the cloud he'd just seen was steam that had escaped while the two men eased inside.

Fargo paused at the counter for long enough to be sure that the clerk's problems weren't going to get worse if he didn't get attention right away.

What the hell was going on in the steam room? Shit. Josiah Abernathy, maybe the richest man in America, was in there, providing that the bodyguard Fargo had met upstairs had been telling the truth. That seemed probable, since the oaf was too dumb to make anything up.

A man like Abernathy could attract all kinds of unwanted attention. Kidnapping seemed most likely. If the two intruders were up to that, then Fargo's best course would be to wait here, his gun ready for their emergence.

But Fargo glumly realized that if Abernathy was like most men who were filthy rich, he'd have accumulated enemies about as fast as he accumulated wealth. So the two men could be vengeful assassins, bent on murder.

A shrill squeal that easily penetrated the thick door made Fargo's mind up for him. He grabbed the latch, a lever rather than a knob, and pulled the heavy door open, staying behind it as it came around. Deftly, he removed his knife from its calf holster.

"What the hell?" somebody shouted.

"Who in hell's out there?" came another voice.

"Is that you, Jed?" A hoarse whisper floated out.

"Keep your goddamn mouth shut, you old goat, or I'll shut it for you. Clem, see what's at the door."

Fargo listened for Clem to clamber to the doorway. When the man's grimy talonlike fingers reached around the edge, Fargo sliced.

Clem yelped as the fog, billowing from the steam room, took on a momentary rose tinge from droplets of blood. It spurted from the base of Clem's fingers and flew in all directions as he thrashed his injured hand.

When Clem began to shuffle forward Fargo eased out a bit, so he had good leverage for an explosive kick. He had hoped to catch Clem's head, but given poor visibility, he was satisfied when his boot slammed into Clem's torso and his ribs cracked like matchsticks.

"Can we get out of here?" the leader grunted from maybe fifteen feet away.

"Sure," Fargo agreed in a pained voice.

The shuffling moved toward the door as Fargo tugged Clem's lean body aside and stepped over behind the counter, where he'd have some cover.

The first man to emerge from the door, and then the mists, sported tremendous salt-and-pepper muttonchop whiskers and a bit of a paunch, which was easy to notice because he wasn't wearing a stitch. It took an instant for Fargo to identify him, but if the man had been wearing tailored broadcloth, he'd look just like those woodcuts in *Harper's Weekly*. Josiah Abernathy appeared surprisingly unflustered for a naked man with a pistol muzzle jammed into the small of his back.

In lock step behind Abernathy was the leader of this afternoon's raid. Huskier than his partner, and a bit taller than Abernathy, he was pushing hard with a revolver. "Move it," he commanded.

"You'll never get away with this, not in broad daylight," Abernathy whispered. "And Jed, my bodyguard, is about. He'll show up any moment now."

"Clem's done took care of him. How much do you reckon your family might pay to get you back?" His voice caught for an instant. "Hey, Clem, where in hell are you?"

Fargo stood and hollered, "Jump!"

Abernathy leapt sideways. His captor swung the pistol toward Fargo, but he never had a chance. Fargo's bullet caught the man square in his gaping mouth. The soft lead expanded as it struck his tonsils. When the bullet emerged in a halo of blood and gristle a moment later, the man had a mouth-sized hole on the back side of his head. He spun once before his knees buckled as he collapsed onto the floor.

"Who are you?" Abernathy demanded as he looked first at Fargo and then around the room for some clothes.

"Skye Fargo. Who were they?"

Abernathy ignored the question. "Where's Jed?"

"Jed about my size, but kind of ruddy all the way around?"

Abernathy nodded.

"He and I had a little disagreement upstairs about how long my bath should last. He'll be fine whenever he wakes up and gets untied."

Abernathy shook his head and sighed. "Hope you don't take that personally, Mr. Fargo. Oh, by the way, I have the advantage of you. Let me introduce myself. I'm Josiah Abernathy." He didn't seem to be in any hurry to come over and sully his soft hands by shaking with the Trailsman, but Fargo let that slide.

"I figured as much," Fargo conceded. "What happened?"

"Even in a private car, one cannot avoid getting covered with cinders and soot on the Hannibal and St. Joseph Railway." Abernathy kept looking around.

Fargo saw some compartments behind the counter, and he figured that's where people's clothes stayed during their fancy steam baths. The first one he opened had Abernathy's clothes, so he stepped aside for the man to come and dress.

The clerk was starting to stir a bit, so Fargo eased him to a more comfortable spot.

"So, several companions and I decided to refresh ourselves with a bath. I sent Jed ahead to secure the premises against just this sort of thing. The clerk assured us all was in order. And then these two miscreants arrived."

Fargo nodded. "And they wanted to kidnap you and hold you for ransom. No mystery there, anyway."

Abernathy looked more disheveled than a fresh-bathed wealthy man ought to, but he seemed less concerned about appearances than about getting out of here soon. "Would you escort me over to my hotel, sir? Immediately?"

"No."

"No? I'll make it well worth your while. I'm staying at the Patee House."

"That's just across the damn street," Fargo grunted. "And there's people all over here, including your damn bodyguard, who need help. We've got to get a doctor and the law."

From the look on Abernathy's face, it had been years since he had heard anyone say "no" to him. He didn't argue, though. He bristled and harrumphed for a few seconds, then stormed out the door. Out its tiny window, Fargo watched, just to make sure the man got across the street in one piece. After that, his first impulse was to head out the door himself and let the survivors in the Alhambra sort things out when they came around.

But the clerk, slumped against a wall, was starting to stir, moaning low and awful about how his head hurt. Fargo assured him he would be back shortly, then legged it upstairs, where Jed the bodyguard was starting to take

27

interest in the visible world. Fargo left the man's hands tied until they got down to the front door, than sent him over to see his boss, with the added instruction to fetch a doctor for the Alhambra.

Fargo found an unconscious man in the closet at the foot of the stairs, and he decided that he had to be the upstairs attendant. The desk clerk was sitting up, with considerable help from the wall at his back. Pale and trembling, he kept shaking his head as he looked around the room. He was still upset even after Fargo hauled Clem into the closet and jammed a chair against the door, for safekeeping until the law showed up.

"What's the problem?" Fargo inquired as the man kept waving, apparently pointing into the steam room.

He tried to talk, but all his earlier glibness was gone. What came out was so mumbled and jumbled that Fargo couldn't make sense out of it. Something about the steam room.

Wait. There had been a shrill scream, like a woman's, right at the start of this ruckus. And Abernathy had said he had companions, hadn't he?

The quickest way to check was to examine the storage compartments where Abernathy's clothes had been. The first one Fargo opened was empty. But the next had a lot of fancy women's duds, as did its neighbor, and those clothes looked just like those that had been on Penelope.

Two expensive women inside the steam room? "Well, hell," Fargo muttered to himself, "if I had more money than God, it's something I'd like to try, too." He pulled the door open, blinked as the steam rolled out, and stepped inside.

Leather-soled boots weren't built for these moist floors, so Fargo took his time. Besides, he couldn't see where he was going. Something hard thumped him high on his shin, just below the knee. Ignoring the resultant throbbing, he bent low and explored with this hands.

It was a polished hardwood bench that seemed to extend all the way along the wall. If this was like the steam room in St. Louis that the Trailsman had once visited, then the bench would run along all four sides, with a gap for the door. Fargo felt along the bench.

Some light struggled in through the door, but it didn't get more than a yard or two, even after the Trailsman's eyes had adjusted. So he continued to feel his way around, and after he turned the corner, what he felt wasn't a mere bench. It felt just like a woman's thigh.

His instincts pushed him two ways. Habit told him to just keep moving his hand up the smooth warm flesh, while wariness demanded that he make sure he knew what he had his hand on, such as whether it was living or dead.

Wariness won, although Fargo didn't mind at all when further groping exploration found a firm breast that pretty well filled his big hand. The tender mound seemed to be rising and falling a bit. Just to be sure, he lowered his head and pressed his ear into the sprawled cleavage. The magnificent body was breathing regularly.

Her hair was short, so this wasn't Penelope, unless Penelope had been wearing a wig outside. On the back of her head, she had a fresh bump the size of a walnut. She must have been in here with Abernathy and gotten knocked out by the intruders.

Fargo lifted her dropped leg up onto the bench, so she'd be more comfortable.

"Mmmm, honey," she murmured as she turned on the bench.

Fargo fixed her location and continued his circuit. He almost scalded his fingers when he got them too close to the steam jets, which hissed in the corner by the door. But he didn't find any other bodies, alive or otherwise.

Shit. He'd have to work his way across the open area in the middle. Recollecting his steps, he judged the room about twelve feet across and fifteen feet deep. Four or five passes should cover it, providing he could go straight. He found the start of the bench and tugged off his boots, so that he wouldn't cause further injuries if he accidentally stepped on somebody. Even his weight might hurt, though, so he decided to get on all fours for his search.

Once he got started, he thought about going out to the lobby and borrowing a coal-oil lamp. But its light likely wouldn't extend any farther than he could feel, anyway, and before he could think much more about it, he heard some labored breaths punctuated by tiny sobs.

Unless he was totally turned around, the sounds weren't coming from the woman on the bench. He crawled toward the sniffles. "Can you hear me, honey?"

Fargo should have figured that any woman who'd just been knocked cold and left on the floor wouldn't be real eager to meet more strangers in the dark. About the time his head was about a foot from her mouth, she shrieked as loudly as a locomotive whistle.

"Penelope?" He tried to keep his voice level and civil.

"Who are you?"

"I'm Skye Fargo," he assured her. "We've met."

"No, we haven't." She started to sit up. One of her arms flailed and raked some wicked fingernails across the Trailsman's forearm. When her head came up, her crown met Fargo's jaw, to their mutual displeasure.

Fargo rolled back and rubbed his bearded chin while he thought for a moment. No wonder she didn't think they'd met. "Penny, honey, you can call me Jethro if it suits you better," he muttered, wondering where she was.

The sigh was audible, and it came right at his side. He probed that way and felt the small of a woman's back nudging down and toward him. When he leaned, what passed his lips was unmistakably a ripe nipple, which just pushed itself into his reflexive kiss. He savored it while

30

one hand dropped to slide along a sleek thigh and the other confirmed that the nipple he tongued was part of a matched pair.

Her hands were busy on their own, getting a grip of sorts on his shoulder blades while she settled atop his lap.

"Just hold me, Jethro, or Skye, or whoever you are," she murmured. Her body slid on downward.

Fargo reluctantly broke his sweet connection with her cherrylike right nipple. He embraced her, his hands joining with the tangle of curls that tumbled below her neck.

"What happened to Mr. Arbuthnot?" she whispered. "Did those two men hurt him?"

Arbuthnot? Poor Penelope. Men just didn't tell her their proper names. Fargo had been suspicious outside, and Josiah Abernathy likely gave a different name because he wanted to avoid the chance of getting black-mailed by some out-of-town fling. There must be things that a man in his position would prefer that his wife didn't hear about, and Abernathy could afford to pay whatever it might take to further his mate's ignorance.

"Mr. Arbuthnot is just fine, Penelope," Fargo consoled. The way she nibbled at his earlobe was more than pleasant, and one of her hands was beneath his shirt. "He's gone back to his hotel room. The two men that came in here won't be bothering anybody again."

"What about Bess? She was in here, too, when they came in."

Fargo shifted to help Penelope tug one sleeve off. "She got bumped on the head, but she seemed to be breathing proper. One of these years, a doctor might get here, so we can be sure."

What Penelope seemed sure of was that Fargo's remaining clothes were in the way. While her lips remained close to his ear, her hands had unbuckled his belt and were unbuttoning his fly. "So, you really are Skye Fargo," she whispered. "I was so sure, because you resembled the description."

This wasn't the time for any thoughtful conversation, not the way his pants seemed to be sliding off all on their own, not with his desire throbbing like a trip-hammer and rising like a smokestack. But he summoned some of his wit as the rest of his clothes came off. "Why would anybody want you to find me, Penny?"

He could feel her shrug from the way her nipples traced his chest. "I don't know," she confessed. "It was Mr. Arbuthnot's idea. He wanted me to find you and, well, talk to you, if you know what I mean. . . ."

Penny tightened the scissors lock that her supple thighs had around Fargo's lower torso. She seemed to float forward, to where the sensitive and yearning tip of his shaft found just the spot it had been lusting for. The muscles in his rump seemed to start flexing all on their own as he began some slow upward thrusts.

When he bothered to think about it, Fargo sorely wished that some backrest was convenient. As it was, he and Penelope teetered back and forth, with his rear as the fulcrum. And since he was bigger, the major part of the swing went his way, which made rocking back something of a chore. But a pleasant one. With every swing her way, he probed deeper into her ardent depths.

"Deeper," she urged, "more."

Fargo obliged her a bit, but it felt too damn good to be hurried along. He slid his hands down from her shoulder blades to the small of her back, allowing her torso to rock more freely. When she leaned rearward to accommodate some more of him, his lips swooped down so that he could nuzzle her heaving breasts, savoring each nipple as it swelled under his searching tongue.

Meanwhile she rocked her hips, trying to sidle forward to engulf some more of the Trailsman. He helped her along by sliding his hands down to her rump, palming a satin cheek in each of his big hands as his fingers kneaded her eager flesh like biscuit dough.

"Oh, God, Skye, now," Penelope gasped, loud enough to attract attention from anybody who might be standing outside the steam room.

Damn. Fargo had gotten so preoccupied that he'd forgot that the door was open, that a doctor and some city police would be arriving any second now. Not to mention the clerk and attendant, who had to be awake enough to hear this.

All good things had to come to an end, so Fargo drove as much as he conveniently could into Penelope. It felt delightful, the way she was rocking and twisting her hips, her internal muscles stroking and squeezing.

The feverish breath panting against his face was hotter than the steam jetting into the room. "Now, now, please, now."

Glad to oblige, Fargo erupted, thrusting upward with not much more than sheer willpower. He wasn't anywhere near all the way in, but such novelty was refreshing. Penelope gave up on gasping and started shouting stuff that didn't make a whole lot of sense, and Fargo was beyond caring what anybody said. He was shuddering a lot himself as spasm after spasm swept across Penelope and squeezed on his shaft.

Each heaving convulsion started deep within her core with a vise clamp that rolled down his rod until the impulse reached the surface, where it split two ways. One jolt shot down her thighs, which seemed certain to bruise his waist if they slammed any tighter. The other upheaval rose up her bosom and poked her nipples into the Trailsman. She pressed her lips against him. Her fingers dug into his back and shoulders.

Once they settled down a bit, Penelope let a hand drop, just so she could check on their dark connection while Fargo was still within her.

"My God, there's more? Is that all for me?"

"No, Penny," Bess announced as her low, husky voice moved up from the wall bench and toward them. "I'd enjoy my share." Some hands materialized that seemed to be urging Fargo to ease back, to lie flat on the floor while Penelope remained mounted atop him.

He didn't argue, although in the dark, moist shuffling that followed, he would have gotten mighty confused if he'd even tried to sort out what belonged to whom. It all felt so good that he didn't even think about trying.

3

The sun was well on its way to providing another scorcher of a day by the time Fargo stepped out of the plush suite Penny and Bess were sharing at the Patee House. He noticed that it was just down the hall from the bigger and plusher suite that Josiah Abernathy was renting.

Once outside, he glanced down the street and saw a clock with a yard-wide face that stood on a post before a jeweler's shop. Ten minutes after nine, which meant the bank would be open. Breakfast could wait. He sniffed and figured he could use another bath. His musky ambience of recent and fervent rutting didn't seem quite proper for a bank, especially the imposing granite-walled Bank of the West.

But another bath could wait, seeing as how yesterday's effort at cleanliness had led to complications that had continued into the evening. The local law was naturally interested in the ruckus at the Alhambra, and squaring that took some time. After that, though, the two high-priced trollops had invited him over to their room for a night of delight that would have cost Abernathy a couple hundred dollars.

Fargo had just finished his business at the bank and was thanking the teller when he saw Josiah Abernathy, the richest man in America, and Alexander Majors emerging from the manager's office. Abernathy paused to thank Fargo again for preventing his kidnapping yesterday. But it was Alexander Majors who was most interested in seeing him. Majors stepped over and started pumping the Trailsman's right hand. "Skye, my old friend, have you got a few minutes to talk?"

Fargo blinked in surprise as his mind whirred and he stared dully at Majors.

Majors sometimes sported a beard, but today his clean-shaven and lean face looked sincere. His thin lips weren't even pinched, the way they usually were.

Alex Majors was a partner in Russell, Majors & Waddell, the biggest freight outfit in the West, likely the world. It was also a company that had never done any business with the Trailsman, on account of Majors' peculiar Sunday-school notions about how employees should conduct themselves.

Fargo couldn't help but be curious as to why Majors was now treating him like a long-lost rich uncle. "Sure, I've got time to talk," Fargo said slowly. "What's on your mind?"

"This must be discussed in privacy," Majors whispered as he gestured toward the front door. Outside, Majors stepped down the street as though he owned St. Joe. A few blocks later, they were in his office at the Pony Express terminal, a sprawling building that was laid out about the same as the usual livery stable, except it was brick.

"Skye, would you go to work for us?" Majors settled into the leather of his padded swivel chair.

"No," Fargo announced. "I came to you a time or two when I was as poor as Job's turkey and needed work bad. And you sons of bitches were too damn upright to hire me as a wagon master, or even as a wrangler. If I wasn't good enough for you then, what makes me good enough now?"

Masters made himself look perplexed. "A man of your talents? And our firm wouldn't engage you?"

"Damn right you wouldn't hire me." Fargo exhaled through pursed lips to blow off some of his rising anger. "Just because I wouldn't lie to you."

Majors shifted uncomfortably and began to blush a bit. "It is certainly not our policy to encourage our employees to take liberties with the truth. In fact, we hire only men of exemplary moral character."

"Bullshit."

Majors winced at the earthy word. "Skye, you can't argue with me about that. Every new employee is issued a bible. They all sign oaths that they will not curse or blaspheme while in our employ. They all swear to observe the Sabbath, and to abstain totally from intoxicating liquors."

Fargo towered above the sitting Majors as his anger rose. "Alex, if a man needs a job bad enough, he'll tell you that he's going to quit cussing, though that's the only known way to get the attention of muleflesh and oxen. He'll promise to read that bible. He'll vow that he'll halt the wagon train all day every Sunday, even if he's on open trail and at a foolish place to stop. He'll pledge to give up liquor. He'll swear to give up women. He might even guarantee that he won't even think about them. Men will say a lot of things if it'll put coins in their pockets and food in their bellies."

"We have our rules," Majors intoned.

"Indeed you do," Fargo granted. "But the point is that once your crews are away from your direct oversight in St. Joe, nobody follows those rules. Your teamsters cuss and carouse and profane the Sabbath with the best of them. I know that and you know that."

Majors shook his head, as if he didn't know that, but Fargo just pressed on.

"And when I saw you about hiring on a couple years ago, you told me all about the rules I'd have to swear to abide by. There wasn't a snowball's chance in hell that

I'd ever follow such rules. I might have been so broke that I couldn't have afforded to shake hands with a two-bit whore, but still I wasn't going to lie to you.

"I told you the plain truth then, same as I'm telling you now: that if you hired me, I'll do the best damn job I can. But I'm not about to make promises that I know I can't keep, and the only way you'd hire me is if I gave you such sham promises. Where I come from, that makes a man a liar."

Majors sighed and shrugged. Fargo, sure that this conversation was over, turned on his heel toward the door.

Majors' plaintive voice halted the Trailsman's long stride. "Skye, I'm willing to let bygones be bygones if you are."

Fargo shrugged. "Still doesn't change the rules you have now."

Majors looked thoughtful for a moment. "Those rules are for employees. If you're agreeable, then we could do business with you as an independent contractor. Those rules wouldn't apply to you any more than they apply to people that sell us wagons or oxen."

Fargo returned to his chair. "Tell me what you need first, and then I'll tell you how agreeable I feel."

"You understand that all of this is confidential?"

Fargo nodded.

"You've got to keep all this under your hat, Skye, and that might be hard for you."

Fargo fought off an attack of rising temper. "What the hell do you mean by that?"

"Don't take offense, Skye. Let me explain." Majors leaned forward. "You know Josiah Abernathy, don't you?"

"Wouldn't say that we're exactly drinking buddies, but I know him."

"Do you know how he makes his money?"

"Speculating on Wall Street," Fargo replied.

"How much do you know about how Wall Street works?"

Fargo mulled for a moment. "Precious little."

"What you need to realize is that stock prices rise and fall, based on what people know. If you learn something a little ahead of everybody else, and you know what effect that news is going to have on the market, then you can make a killing."

Fargo's eyes remained narrow.

"You were just part of an example, Skye. Those mines in the Rockies are owned by joint-stock corporations with investors. The price of shares of stock goes up and down, depending on how much gold the mines are producing."

"Stands to reason," Fargo agreed.

"When those mines ran into refractory ores that they couldn't refine with their primitive stamp mills, then the stock prices dropped. If you'd known that a little ahead of time, you could have sold their stock short and made a tidy profit when the news got to Wall Street."

"Sell short?"

"Okay, suppose United Blackhawk Mines stock is selling for ten dollars a share. You find out early that they've run out of easy ore. You know the price is going to drop to about two dollars a share once word gets out, which will happen sometime next week. So you sell it short. You'll offer United Blackhawk shares for nine dollars. Since the market price at the moment is ten, you've got all kinds of takers."

Fargo started to see the possibilities. "It takes a few days for the paperwork to settle, I suppose. So you sell all this stock you don't have, but that doesn't matter. The buyers have agreed to take it off your hands at nine dollars. And when they have to take delivery on that stock, a few days have passed. The news is out, the market has dropped. You can buy all the United you want for two dollars, and those poor bastards have to buy it from you for nine dollars." The Trailsman concluded with a low whistle of appreciation.

Majors confirmed Fargo's theorizing. "That's precisely how it works, Skye. On Wall Street, information is money. Abernathy is interested in United Blackhawk. He wanted to know the moment that the ore arrived here—or if it didn't, on account of an Indian raid or the like.

"Since it got here, he'll telegraph his agents and brokers to start buying all the United they can find. When the news of the successful shipment reaches the rest of Wall Street in a few days, the stock will rise. Abernathy will sell it then. He'll make a couple hundred thousand dollars. If the shipment hadn't gotten through, he could have sold United short. Either way, he makes money as long as he's the first to know."

"Shit," Fargo muttered as it became clear to him why Penelope had been so eager to find the Trailsman and then chat with him while she bedded him. He hadn't made any secret of his freighting job, but then again, the men who'd hired him hadn't said anything about staying quiet. All they'd cared about was speed. Fargo knew he could keep a secret when it was necessary; the trick was to know when it was necessary.

"My men and I are the ones who did all the real work," Fargo complained, "and I came out about five hundred dollars ahead. My men didn't even do that well. Guess that shows you who's important these days."

Majors' face grew even longer as he agreed. "It does seem criminal that you go out and risk your life doing real work just to get a few dollars, while men like Abernathy, men who don't do any sort of real work, somehow come up with millions. I tell you, this country is bound straight for perdition if this continues. Things will have to change."

"I wouldn't hold my breath." Fargo eased back and got comfortable, now that he and Majors seemed to be getting along. "We just wandered all over Robin Hood's barn, talking about how information makes some men richer. As I recollect, that all started when you wanted to impress on me how important it was to be discreet."

"And now you're wondering what you're supposed to be discreet about?"

At Fargo's nod, Majors explained his problems, which were at least as complicated as the workings of a pocket watch. The gist of it was that the company had been in a financial bind, and the only good way to ease the pinch was to get the government contract for hauling overland mail to the West Coast—a contract worth about $600,000 a year.

Right now, the Butterfield Overland Mail Company held the lucrative contract. John Butterfield's wagons started in St. Louis and swung south to Fort Smith, then west into the Indian Nations before crossing Texas to El Paso. After that came a lot more desert—Fort Tucson, Yuma, San Diego. And since most Californians lived in the mining regions, the mail then had to go six hundred miles north to San Francisco.

Butterfield's route was fantastically indirect, and worse than dangerous with its deserts, Comanche, and eight or nine varieties of Apache. Years ago, Fargo had ridden guard on that run for a few months.

Russell, Majors & Waddell wanted to get the mail contract away from Butterfield, and as Majors explained it, they had a good shot at it because the route they would use was considerably shorter. A variant of the familiar California Trail, it ran in pretty much a straight line from civilization to San Francisco. It followed the Platte across the Great Plains, eased around the Rockies at South Pass, and wiggled across the desert from Great Salt Lake City to the Sierras.

"But the problem is that Aaron Brown, the postmaster general who decides such matters, is a southerner," Majors continued. "He's from country where it hardly ever snows, so he's sure that our central route would be blocked by blizzards for half the year. That's why he keeps giving the contract to Butterfield, who's got a route where it's warm year 'round."

To change the postmaster general's mind, Russell, Majors & Waddell had launched the Pony Express last spring. If it could run all year and keep its breakneck schedule of ten days from St. Joe to San Francisco, then the government would have to agree that the central route was not only shorter, but eminently practical as a year 'round mail route.

"I did wonder why anybody'd bother to go to all that expense and trouble," Fargo interjected, "because I couldn't see any way that your Pony Express could come close to paying for itself. But it's all starting to make sense, now."

"And you're still wondering what I have in mind for you." If Majors had been a smoker, he would have lit a cigar. As it was, he laced his fingers and popped his knuckles before proceeding. "Skye, Abernathy was putting a lot of pressure on me today. He'd like to buy the Pony Express."

"From what you said, it isn't his kind of investment, since it isn't a paying proposition at the moment."

Majors lifted and dropped his round shoulders. "That's one thing that puzzles me, too. Maybe he knows something I don't. But the point is that he had a complaint, and if I don't act quickly upon his complaint, then he's going to belittle us all over Wall Street, and that will drive us under."

"How?" Fargo wondered. "You, Russell, and Waddell are a partnership, aren't you? You're not a corporation where he could juggle your stock prices."

"Even partnerships have to borrow money," Majors explained. "And if Abernathy doesn't like you, your credit rating goes straight to perdition, while the interest you pay on your notes goes straight the other way. But there is more to it than that. Abernathy says that several dispatches from the West Coast that were addressed to him have been delayed. Understand that a great deal of our Pony Express business is correspondence to and from Manhattan financiers when they deal with the West Coast. If Abernathy starts telling everybody that the Pony Express isn't reliable, then we shall lose that business. And without that business, we sink."

"Just where do I fit in?" Fargo asked.

The answer was what he expected. "I want you to start here and head west, until you find out how Abernathy's messages are being delayed. And then I want you to take appropriate action to prevent it from recurring."

"You're sure they're being delayed?" Fargo's suspicions were mounting. "If Abernathy wants to buy the Pony Express, then maybe he's making all this up so that you'll get even more pinched and want to sell to him, fast and at a cheap price."

"The thought crossed my mind, too," Majors granted. "But he showed me several envelopes that convinced me to the contrary." Majors reached into an inside pocket of his frock coat and presented Fargo with three empty envelopes.

For easier reading, the Trailsman stepped over to the office's tiny window.

The top right corner of the topmost envelope had a regular government ten-cent postage stamp, with its engraved portrait of George Washington. That was canceled, just like other mail. On the left side, above the address, was the Pony Express cachet, an egg-shaped oval about two inches long. Inside, the words "PONY EXPRESS" pressed against the top of the curve, and "SAN FRANCISCO" the bottom. There was enough room between the two for a line drawing of a galloping steed, its tail flying behind it, and a date.

The date was May 11. Fargo consulted the rolled-back

pages of the flyspecked calendar on the wall next to the window, and saw that May 11 had been a Friday, which was the day the weekly Pony Express left San Francisco.

When it got to St. Joe, the letter was transferred from the private Pony Express into the government postal system. It had cost ten dollars to get the message from San Francisco to St. Joe. The rest of the trip, from St. Joe to New York via rail, cost only a ten-cent George Washington stamp.

This dispatch should have arrived in St. Joe in ten days, on May 21. Even May 22 would be understandable. But the St. Joe postmark across the postage stamp was dated May 28.

Fargo examined the other two envelopes. Both had also been delayed for a week, somewhere between San Francisco and St. Joe. He turned to Majors. "I guess there's no arguing with that."

Majors shook his head. "I'm afraid not. There is indeed a problem. Do you believe you can solve it?"

"I told you earlier that I don't make promises I know I can't keep. And there isn't a man on earth who could promise to find and cure any problem that's lurking somewhere along two thousand miles of prairie, mountain, desert, Pawnee, Lakota, Cheyenne, Shoshoni, Paiute, and Diggers, not to mention a hundred and fifty of your stations, all with agents and stock tenders, and the fifty or so riders you've got—that's a lot of country and people to be looking into. But I'll give it my best shot."

Majors offered a handshake, which Fargo accepted. "Your best is good enough for me, Skye, because if you can't do something, then I don't believe it can be done. Just remember to keep this quiet. If word gets out that we're even looking into a problem with delayed messages, then Russell, Majors, and Waddell will be finished."

Once outside, the Trailsman blinked at the sunshine and realized he didn't have the vaguest notion of where he should start.

4

After a week of poking east and a bit north from St. Joe, the Trailsman knew he was getting close to the line between Kansas and Nebraska territories.

He had learned plenty about how the Pony Express operated. About every dozen miles, there was a station where the riders changed mounts, flinging their *mochilas* from one saddle to the next. Thus they always rode fresh horses, which they pushed at a hell-bent gallop. Every fifty miles or so was a bigger station where riders were changed. Such stations had lodging, where a rider stayed until the *mochila* going the other way arrived. Then he galloped back to where he had started.

Every station had at least a horse corral and a shack for the stock tender. But most offered more. The Pony Express followed the same course as the main route of Central Overland California & Pikes Peak Express Co., which was also owned by Russell, Majors & Waddell. So about half the Pony Express facilities were also stage stops.

The lodging was often the packed-dirt floor of the main room. Stage passengers spread their bedrolls under a leaking roof and squirmed until sunrise to a serenade of snores. Sometimes women got that room, while men were sent to the barn.

The overpriced food was even worse. It cost a whole fifty cents for a plate of greasy doughnuts, foul-smelling eggs, and putrid bacon. All of it had a greenish tinge and was appetizing only to the clouds of ravenous flies that buzzed around the encrusted tin plates.

After crossing the Missouri last week and heading into Kansas Territory, Fargo found the same nauseating pattern at every dismal stop—Elwood, Cold Springs, Troy, Kennekuk, Granada, Log Chain, Seneca, Guittard's, and Marysville.

At the Hollenberg station this morning, the coffee had at least been the real item, instead of the usual tepid mixture of spent grounds, chicory root, and burnt corn. But it was so weak that a stage passenger, after observing that no ladies sat with them at the splintered table, had turned to the Trailsman.

"This coffee reminds me of making love in a canoe," the husky young man whispered.

After speculating for a few moments and coming up with no resemblance between the two, Fargo took the bait. "How's that?"

"It's fucking near water."

The lad had been right enough about that, but Fargo felt sufficiently awake as the Ovaro's ground-eating trot took him up yet another rise. The road ran parallel to the Little Blue River, never more than a couple of miles away. The farther west Fargo went, the more sparse were the trees, and here almost all the wood grew close by the river, which often ran between low chalky bluffs. The trail crossed rolling country sweltering under a summer sun that was never all that bright, due to a persistent haze.

Fargo reined up and dismounted so he could drain another bladder of the feeble coffee he had swilled so much of a couple hours ago. The next stop would be Rock Creek, the first station in Nebraska Territory, and it couldn't be far.

Staying at the stations had given Fargo plenty of opportunity to watch what went on and to talk to the help. But it hadn't told him much.

Most stock tenders couldn't do much more than grunt when asked a question. Their homely women, who handled the kitchen duties, weren't exactly garrulous, either. But although most of them appeared to be about as ignorant as so many oxen, they weren't so stupid that they'd say anything like "Well, yes, Mr. Fargo, I have been tampering with the dispatches in those Pony Express pouches."

Fargo had to admit that he had no more idea of where to find the Pony Express problem than he had when he'd ridden out of St. Joe. He needed to try a different tack.

This time around, Fargo figured he would camp by the station and observe from outside. The country here was reasonably settled, with farmsteads dotting the landscape. He'd try talking to some of the neighbors. Country folks tended to gossip an awful lot, so he might have a chance of hearing a useful tidbit.

Fargo and the Ovaro splashed across the ford of Rock Creek, a shallow Little Blue tributary that was only three or four yards wide. The road climbed out of the mud and brush along the banks. Only a furlong ahead, the station was just a log cabin, maybe twenty feet square, with one slab door and one tiny window. Next to it sat the corral, with a stable that dwarfed the station.

Fargo didn't plan on staying there, but it made sense to stop first before visiting the neighbors. He tied his big pinto to a rail of the corral fence, then wandered into the stable with the improbable hope that this stock tender would be more coherent than the others.

Fargo had an inch or two on the young man he found cleaning dank straw out of a stall. Clad in buckskins, the gent looked strong and husky. When he turned, the Trailsman saw a man in his early twenties. His face was broad but not well-proportioned. His pale-blue eyes sat too close together, his ears stuck out like jug handles despite his shoulder-length blond hair, his chin seemed to vanish, and above it, his upper lip protruded like a duck's bill.

Despite his broad shoulders, his hands were tiny. He winced when he moved his left arm to set the pitchfork down and extended his right to shake with Fargo. "Want to stable your horse, mister?" he inquired.

"Likely not," the Trailsman responded. "Just wondering where I might camp nearby. Now that you mention it, though, my pinto could use a rubdown and some grain this afternoon."

"Bring him in, then." The young man glanced down the hall between the stalls to the open door. "I'll have time before the stage arrives, but once it rolls in, it's all assholes and elbows until we finish tending to it."

They fetched the Ovaro, and Fargo couldn't help but notice how much the hostler favored his left arm as he began to remove the pinto's heavy saddle.

"Let me help you with that," Fargo offered.

The response was a grunt and a fierce shaking of the head. "No, I can do it. Just stand back. Damn this left arm of mine."

Fargo figured he'd do as asked, but since the stock tender had brought up the subject, it was fair to inquire about the arm while the pained man slowly went about his work. "I've bunged up an arm a time or two myself," the Trailsman commented. "Guess you never know how much you use a part of you, even your left arm, until you hurt it and the pain grabs you every time you think about moving it."

"That's for damn sure." He had finished untying the latigo from the clinch and was now steeling himself to grab the horn and cantle to pull the saddle off. "I should have known better."

"Better than what?"

Now the gent had a chance to brag between clenched-teeth gasps, so he took it. "Better than to take on a grizzly sow with just a bowie knife and a brace of pistols."

Fargo thought he might have heard of this, since there was a tale about such that was making its rounds through the freighter fraternity. "Did that happen last fall, clear over on Raton Pass?"

The man nodded.

"You must be Jim Hickok." Fargo stepped back as the man pulled the blanket off the Ovaro and grabbed a currycomb.

The man nodded again. "Yeah, that's me, all right. Was driving a freight wagon to Santa Fe for good old Alex Majors. Comanche were fractious then, so the Cimarron Cutoff wasn't a good notion. We took the mountain branch over Raton Pass. Up in the trees, this damned old grizzly sow and her two cubs were squatting right in the middle of the road."

"Imagine that pretty well stalled your mules," Fargo urged. The story wasn't that exciting, but the man seemed to take such pleasure in telling it that Fargo was willing to appear eager to listen. Besides, if Hickok just kept talking, there was always a chance that he'd say something interesting.

"Yeah, my brutes weren't about to take another step. I hollered some and waved my hat, but those bears weren't about to move, neither. Jumped off the wagon and waved my guns some, thinking maybe that would persuade Mama Bear to get off the road. But she just sat there, her and her two cubs. So I got close and sent a bullet into her."

Stupid. That's what Hickok had been. Grizzlies had tough hides and were huge. The only sure way to take one down was a direct shot through the eye socket with a big gun like a Sharps. Lobbing pistol balls at a grizzly sow would just aggravate her.

Hickok finished grooming the Ovaro's near side. He clucked some to soothe the horse, then stepped around to the sweaty far side before continuing.

"Hell, that big old sow didn't even notice the first slug. By about the fourth one, though, she got plenty riled. So she charged me. I emptied both pistols, and I misdoubt it even slowed her down enough to matter."

Fargo recalled his encounter with a grizzly that had produced a big scar on his left arm, and he leaned back against the stable wall. "Surprised you lived through it," he prodded.

"No bullets left, and she was atop me. You've never smelled nothin' as horrid as a grizzly's breath."

"Even the food they serve at these stage stations?"

Hickok laughed. "The chow's bad, but nothin's that bad. She got her paws around me, clamped me so tight I couldn't hardly breathe. Reckon that's why they call it a bear hug. I thought I was a goner, for sure, especially when she started to chew on me. But I did have my bowie knife, and I got her killed before she finished nibbling off my arm."

"And then you walked away?" Fargo gave Hickok more chances to brag.

"Don't I wish. No, I was passed out in the road, with that she-bear's carcass atop me. Matt Farley was driving a wagon about a mile behind. He found me and dragged me out. Down to Santa Fe first; then, when I was able, I got hauled to Kansas City so I could mend some more. The company sent me over here to work at the stables till my arm heals entire and I can go back to freighting." Hickok smiled broadly. "What's your line of work?"

"About the same as what you did before you met the bear," Fargo replied. "And whatever comes up along the way. You know how that goes."

Hickok hung up the currycomb and started out of the stall, Fargo behind him. Once they were out, he examined Fargo closely. "Damn if you don't look like the Trailsman."

"Your eyes work just fine," Fargo replied. "Want to see my bear scar?"

Hickok laughed, but he got out no more than a couple guffaws before his face started falling.

Fargo turned and saw a shorter man, barrel-shaped and sporting a full sandy beard, step into the stable. "Hey, Duck Bill," he commanded. "Get your sorry ass in gear. We pay you to work, not to lollygag."

Hickok reddened, and his upper lip stuck out even more as he stepped sideways, so he could face his boss directly. "David McCanles, you worthless son-of-a-bitch station agent, you know goddamn well how much I hate to be called Duck Bill."

Hand on his Colt, Fargo stepped back. This wasn't his problem, and nobody had invited him to join. But leaving now wasn't real prudent, either. Fargo hoped they'd just holler at each other.

"Duck Bill," McCanles intoned, stretching out each word for maximum effect on Hickok's rising temper, "best you recall that the company has some considerable rules against cussing the way you do. And we've also got rules against loafing. So . . ."

His ranting was interrupted by Hickok's furious charge. The young hostler bulled into McCanles, planting his head into the older man's ribs, rolling him backward. Hickok got in a swift kick at his boss's prone, thrashing torso, but it had about as much effect as his shots had had on that grizzly sow. All that happened was that McCanles rolled sideways and got to his feet while Hickok tried another futile kick.

Flailing with his fists, McCanles lunged at Hickok and caught the younger man's jaw with a roundhouse right. Hickok's head rocked back as blood began to spout from a cut lip. He raised his right arm and jabbed, but McCanles dodged the thrusts and sidestepped.

Hickok's left arm wasn't good for much of anything, including defense. McCanles delivered several swift punches to the stablehand's ribs. Unable to absorb much more of this, Hickok turned in order to bring his good arm into the fight.

McCanles grabbed Hickok's right forearm and twisted, ignoring several thigh-bruising kicks. He intensified the pressure. Hickok thrashed with his left. Despite efforts that made pain flash across his face, Hickok couldn't move his left arm enough to wipe the blood-lust grin off McCanles' face. The few times Hickok's fist did arrive, it landed with the force of a housefly.

With a savage thrust, McCanles rose from his crouch and got his right arm around Hickok's throat, encircling it with the crook of his elbow. He waltzed around the hostler, still clamping Hickok's good arm, which he jammed against the man's back and twisted.

No man could stand up for long against that kind of pressure. From a dozen feet away, Fargo caught Hickok's eye and gave him a look that said, "I'll step in and try to break this up if you want me to."

To the Trailsman's relief, Hickok's negative grimace told Fargo to stay out of this. Moments later, McCanles threw Hickok to the ground, then stepped back.

"Hear me, you worthless duck-billed, jug-eared stable boy. Maybe I don't got nothin' to say 'bout who the company sends to work under me. But as long as I'm the agent and you're the stock tender, then when I say 'frog,' you better jump. And, boy, I'll call you Duck Bill anytime I feel like it. Got that straight? Or do you need another lesson about who's boss around here?"

Hickok still glowered with a burning rage as he lay flat in the muck of the stable floor and caught his breath.

McCanles turned to the Trailsman. "What's your business here, mister? Or did you just come in to listen to that braggart's tall stories?"

Fargo waited to answer until he could see that McCanles was getting edgy. "Came by to get my horse tended. And to see where I might camp hereabouts."

"Camp? Why would a man want to camp when we've got a station house where you've got a roof and your meals all cooked for you?"

"I have my reasons," Fargo replied softly, hoping that he wouldn't end up in a fight with McCanles. He could doubtlessly take the burly station agent, but McCanles was strong and fast enough to make the process painful before Fargo came out on top.

Besides, Fargo had better things to do than fight with moody station agents and their boastful but touchy hired help. Such as figure out who was tampering with the Pony Express, and both of these men bore watching. "So do you know of a nearby place I might camp for a couple days?" Fargo asked.

McCanles looked over his shoulder to make sure Hickok was still relatively inert. "Most of the ground around here is all taken up, mister. Ain't like farther west, where you'd have to work at it to find some private property. Lemme think for a minute."

His thinking was apparent in his face. His first thought was to go over and kick Hickok a few times, until his eyes flitted back to Fargo's imposing stare. McCanles decided against any more torment. Then the agent eyed a mental map and paused at a spot.

"Every bit of land I can think of around here belongs to somebody," McCanles explained, his voice growing more reasonable. "But most farmers would let you camp on their land if you asked."

Fargo had already figured that much, so he thanked McCanles and started over toward his Ovaro.

"Wait just a minute. Your best bet might be the Widow

McCall, just a piece down the road. She's got a few acres, and she ain't farmin' 'em. Her boys are too small to do her much good on a farm. I've heard tell that she'll take in traveling men like yourself." He winked and cackled with that announcement.

A widow who occasioned gossip might well know some, so Fargo figured she was worth finding, whether she offered a camping spot or not. A few minutes later, he turned in his saddle and spotted a ramshackle log house with a long porch and two dirty boys scuffling in front.

The smaller was on top, his hands around the bigger boy's neck. He looked about nine or ten.

"Lemme go, Andy," the bottom one gasped. His voice was in the middle of changing, so the bigger had to be twelve or thirteen. He tried to poke his fingers into the younger brother's eyes.

"Ouch," the upper one hollered, not caring that Fargo was watching. "You're a cockeyed dumbbell, Jack. That's why I'm not gonna let go till you say 'uncle.' "

They continued with even more vigor. Fargo was getting bored with watching other people fight, so he dismounted and stepped over to them.

The two youngsters were oblivious until he cleared his throat as he loomed above them. "Would you two be the McCall boys?"

Wide-eyed, both released their grips and scrambled to their feet. The older one, who must be Jack, spoke first. "Why, yes, sir, we answer to that." He got real interested in staring at his shuffling bare feet, likely because he felt embarrassed by the uncontrolled way that one of his eyes shifted and crossed.

Andy, the younger, stared Fargo up and down. "Why, mister, you're big, even bigger than Duck Bill down at the stable."

Fargo glared at the sassy kid. "I just saw him, and he didn't take real kind to being called Duck Bill."

Undeterred, Andy piped that Hickok was just a big blowhard, and he wasn't one bit scared of Duck Bill. He added that he also wasn't one bit scared of Fargo.

But he was polite and didn't come up with any disgusting nicknames when Fargo asked if the boys' mother was about and whether she'd be upset if he knocked on her door to ask about laying his bedroll on her property. Both Andy and Jack assured him that would be fine with them.

Having cleared this with the men of the house, the Trailsman stepped toward the door. It opened before he got there, and the Widow McCall stepped onto her porch.

Her dark hair was braided and piled atop her head. Attired in a splattered apron that pretty well covered her nondescript frock, she was fairly plump. Not quite fat, but another ten or fifteen pounds would push her over the edge. She was handsome more than she was pretty, a solid, dependable-looking woman.

"Who are you and what do you want?" she asked.

That was a fair question, so Fargo answered.

"So McCanles sent you to see me for a place to lay your bedroll, did he?"

Fargo nodded. "That he did. If he sent me wrong, just shake your head and we'll say no more about it. I'll go on my way."

"You can camp there if you wish." She pointed to a stand of trees close to the creek. "You're welcome to our pen for your horse. And if you care to sup with us, I'd expect some contribution from you."

"Cash or chores?"

She shook her head indifferently. "Whatever suits you best."

Fargo handed her a silver dollar and said he'd be by for breakfast in the morning. He set up camp as he fended off inquiries and insults from Andy and Jack. He wasn't going to eat with them tonight. He didn't tell them that he was going to hang around the station, just to see what he could pick up during dinner after the stage rolled in.

Fargo could barely stomach the food at the station. The only thing filthier than the plates was the manure pile in back. The meat was fried beyond recognition, to the consistency of boot leather, with a smothering taste to match. The stage passengers hardly talked, and when they did, it was understandable that they were complaining.

One of them was a slender young woman with bright-brown eyes, an animated face, and chestnut hair. For a while, just her presence brightened the dinner. But when he caught her eye, she shot him a look that said, "Get lost. You're just another of these uncouth ruffians."

Sometime after midnight, Fargo awakened. Was it a sound? He listened expectantly, but heard only the rumble of his own churning stomach. He had managed dog meat in an Arapaho tepee, raw and dripping buffalo liver with the Comanche, and teeth-shattering army hardtack. Those had never given him such complications. But this stage-station chow made his belly feel like he'd just swallowed an angry mule that was trying to kick its way out.

Fargo pulled himself up and swore this was the last time he'd ever eat in a stage station. His innards churned again and he almost swore that he'd never eat again, if it might lead to this. After another cramping spasm, he decided that if he planned to live through the night, he was going to have to settle his stomach.

His saddlebags lay close to his bedroll, and there was enough of a moon to simplify seeing. He found his pint flask of whiskey. He tipped up the flask and poured about half of it down. The whiskey burned his raw throat, but the warmth began to settle in and he figured he had at least a hope of living till morning.

When he started to lift the flask again, he heard a door move over at the McCall house, fifty yards away. He froze and stared. But it was just Mrs. McCall walking his way. She crossed the ground between them with a determined step.

She halted in front of him for a moment. Fargo rose expectantly. She stepped closer and slid her hand along his waist, her fingers moving to a part of Fargo that was already starting to respond by standing to attention.

He figured fair was fair, so he rested his hand on one of her shoulders. She twisted a bit, not to get away from him but to reveal that she wasn't wearing a stitch under her threadbare robe. Her over-full breasts with dark nipples stood up as though they were begging for consideration. His fingers slid down and caressed them.

"Oh, Mr. Fargo," she sighed. "Do you know how lonely a widow woman can get?" She pressed herself against him, her dark and shadowed pubic thatch finding his thigh.

"Maybe as lonely as men get on the trail?" he offered.

"At least that lonely." She lifted her face, expecting a kiss, and Fargo didn't disappoint her as they sank to the ground. Mrs. McCall spread herself atop the Trailsman's bedroll, her fleshy thighs wide to invite him into her moist cavern of pleasure. She was already bouncing.

Fargo shed his balbriggans. He slid atop her, stopping to savor the ruby-red nipples atop her succulent breasts. His tongue found one, and then the other, darting across the hard tips of flesh.

"Hurry," she urged breathlessly. "I can't leave the boys alone for very long."

Fargo smothered her worries with another kiss, and when she rocked up to meet his yearning shaft, he plunged in deep without further ado.

"Great God," she exclaimed. "I've waited so long!"

She was pillow-soft and easy on his trail-weary bones, but not so easy on his throbbing shaft. She lunged up, demanding every inch Fargo had to offer, something not every woman did. "Yes, oh, yes," she panted. "I want it all."

Her muscles closed around him, hot and greedy. Fargo slid his hands down to her cushioned rump and began to thrust in comfortable, easy rhythm. "Mmn, mmn" the widow moaned from the back of her throat. Then, with each thrust, the tone of her voice rose a little higher, until she was shrieking, "Yes, oh, yes!"

Most often, his chest was close enough to muffle her shouts. But when he moved his hands forward and lifted his torso for a better angle, there wasn't anything to stop her excited shrieks from rising into the night. When they both arrived at glory together, Fargo thought his eardrums would shatter.

5

As the Ovaro trotted away from Rock Creek, Fargo thought about how little information Mrs. McCall had to give him about the Rock Creek station, and how generous she'd been otherwise. It had been a satisfying, if unproductive stop. He saw the usual run of travelers, mostly local folks going about their business.

By summer, there weren't any emigrant trains this far east—they left in April or early May, just as soon as the blizzards gave up for the season and the grass started to green. Fargo met two eastbound freight trains and had coffee with them while talking to the wagon masters, both men he knew. They advised that the summer of 1860 looked to be a dry scorcher along the Platte, and that the Kiowa were riled up. But the Lakota, Cheyenne, and Arapaho seemed peaceful this year.

Talk was that, far to the west, on the sunset side of Utah Territory, the Paiute were raising four kinds of hell, not just attacking travelers, but going after stations in massed raids. Fargo hoped he'd get this job done before he had to go that far.

The stagecoaches rumbled through, one each day bound each way. The same slender Pony Express rider passed, first westbound, then, the next day, eastbound with a different *mochila*. In a week of easy riding, Fargo stopped at each station—Big Sandy, Thompson's, Kiowa, Little

Blue, Liberty Farm, Lone Tree, Thirty-two Mile Creek, and finally Summit.

Summit sat at the top of the divide between the Little Blue and the Platte. Past there, the trees stopped and the bleak sand hills took over. Along with occasional protruding rock formations like Chimney Rock and Scott's Bluff, the hills would dominate the landscape for the next three hundred miles westward to Fort Laramie.

The next station was Fairfield. Fargo spent the night there, on account of a thunderstorm that had started boiling late in the afternoon. He didn't learn anything new.

Between it and Hook's the next day, he passed a halted freight train. It was noon, so the stop was understandable, but the oxen stood chained in their yokes while men rearranged the wagon loads. He knew it was a Russell, Majors, & Waddell train, because the men were cussing so loud that he heard their oaths long before he saw the wagons.

Up near the front, the Trailsman found the wagon master, a short dark-haired and full-bearded man named Jake Wolcott, and inquired of him.

Although they were more than passing acquaintances, Wolcott eyed him suspiciously before deciding Fargo could be trusted. "We're hauling army supplies," he explained. "Last night's rain got into some of the flour," he explained.

"So you're tossing out what's spoiled before it can spoil the rest?" That made sense.

"Don't I wish," Wolcott grunted. "That'd be the honest way to do it. But I got orders from ol' Billy Russell himself. Any flour that's spoiled, we move to the bottom of the load. Which is what we're doin' here."

At Fargo's puzzled look, Wolcott went on, getting more shamefaced by the minute. "Put it on bottom, and it should pass inspection at Kearny. Then we can haul it on to Laramie. If it don't pass that inspection, then the company won't get paid."

Fargo tried to shake off the revulsion he felt. "You mean you've got direct orders to sneak rotten flour to the soldiers?"

Wolcott nodded. "It is kind of sickening, when you put it that way. But what's a man supposed to do? I'd be even lower than them if I quit right here and didn't get the train in. When Billy gave me those instructions before we started, I just hoped it wouldn't come to this. And now, that stuff is going to be full of worms and maggots by the time it gets to Laramie."

"Couldn't you just tell them the truth at Kearny?" Fargo wondered aloud.

"Maybe." Wolcott shrugged. "But then I'd get on the blacklist, and nobody'd hired me. Russell, Majors, Waddell—they all talk pious as preachers, but I've met sidewinders I'd trust more than the whole lot of 'em. Shit, Fargo, you're goddamn lucky you never hired on with them. Maybe you missed some work, but you never got caught up in their lies, neither."

After that, Fargo wasn't about to announce his current employer, even if his mission hadn't been secret. As he rode on, he didn't even bother to stop at Hook's Station. He felt like quitting. Any company that would put its men up to what Wolcott had been doing was no outfit he wanted to work for.

But then again, Wolcott cussed plenty and drank hard and didn't pay any mind to the Sabbath on his travel schedule. Yet to get hired, he had promised to be such a good boy, knowing damn well he wasn't going to be once he was on the job. Men who'd tell lies like that shouldn't mind being ordered to practice deception—Wolcott didn't have any right to much of the indignation he was displaying.

And besides, Fargo had given his word to Majors that

he'd take on this job. Just because Majors and his partners stretched honesty past the breaking point, that was no excuse for him to go back on his word.

But. On the other hand. Then again. Besides. Come to think of it. However. Even so. The whole mess churned in Fargo as the Ovaro plodded toward the setting sun. There didn't seem to be any right way to do what was right here, or even any way to figure out what was right. Fargo didn't want to feel disgusted with himself for working for Majors, but he knew he'd feel just as disgusted if he quit in the middle of a job he said he'd do.

The job? What job was he doing? He hadn't seen a damn thing at any of the stations that indicated dispatches were being delayed.

They had all been good places to eat and get deathly sick, however, so Fargo felt happier than usual to see Fort Kearny's flagpole shimmering in the distance. Since he'd been eating on his own, and because hunting was an exercise in futility along this well-used trail, his supplies were getting low. The sutler at Kearny always kept a good inventory, because it was the last place to stock up before Fort Laramie, better than three hundred hard miles away.

On the south bank of the Platte and foolishly situated in the bottom lands where a good spring flood might carry it away someday, Fort Kearny was certainly an army post, but it didn't look much like a fort. There were no walls, only buildings that faced all four sides of a parade ground.

A line of new telegraph poles extended northeast, along the river toward Council Bluffs. If the telegraph worked the way folks said it did, sending messages for hundreds of miles in the blink of an eye, then it was going to put the Pony Express out of business once the wires got strung clear across the country.

After stabling the Ovaro, Fargo ambled over to the

store. Ben Crenshaw ran it, and he and the Trailsman had come to know each other fairly well, considering that Fargo passed through a lot of different places and that Crenshaw dealt with a lot of different people.

The store's peak business was in May, when the emigrants came through. Today business was slow, so the husky gray-bearded man had no help behind the counter.

"Hell's bells, it's Fargo." Crenshaw put down his feather duster and reached out to shake hands.

"How are things, Ben?" Fargo accepted the handshake. He needed to talk to somebody, to think out loud for a few minutes, and then maybe he'd know what to do about this job. The more he thought about it, the more perplexing it got.

"Fine as frog's hair."

"That must be mighty fine indeed, since it's so fine nobody's ever seen it," Fargo rejoined, feeling better already. "I've got to stock up."

"For how long?" Crenshaw was an experienced frontier storekeeper. All Fargo had to say was, "Fort Laramie, just me on horseback," and Crenshaw would come up with the right amount of parched corn, jerky, hardtack, powder, balls, caps, and other necessities.

"Have it all ready for you in the morning, 'less'n you're in a hurry now."

"Morning's fine," Fargo assured. "Chance you're free this evening?"

"Got plans for the usual weekly poker game, but you'd certainly be welcome, Skye. And it generally breaks up early. Most of the others are soldiers with reveille bugling at them before sunup."

Good. Fargo would have a chance to talk. And if that newfangled telegraph was working, he could wire his resignation to Majors, should that be what he decided. "Guess I'll get some supper, then find you."

"Game starts at seven in the officers' club." Crenshaw

glanced up at the pendulum clock as Fargo started out. "Fargo, wait a second. I damn near forgot."

He halted. "Forgot what?"

"Forgot to tell you that there was a telegram waiting for you. They passed me word to tell you if I saw you. Came in yesterday."

"Where do I find it?"

"Telegraph office is next to the post office, behind the headquarters building across the square. Just follow the wire."

The telegraph office seemed to be a mixture of civilian and military. Behind the counter, one clerk wore jeans and flannel, and the other a corporal's uniform. The soldier came to the counter. "Sir?"

Fargo identified himself. The soldier handed him a flimsy half-sized piece of paper with scrawled letters. He stepped to the front window for better light.

The message was from Majors. It asked him to please report if he'd found anything, or even if he hadn't. It also asked him if he'd do whatever he could to assist one Jennifer Blake.

"Anybody know a Jennifer Blake?" Fargo inquired.

The corporal smiled. "Not as well as I'd like to."

"Mind telling me who she is?"

He glanced at his clock. "She should be by in a couple minutes to see if we've got anything for her."

"Guess I can wait."

Fargo advised Majors by a collect telegraph that he was at Fort Kearny and hadn't seen anything suspicious. He was going to add that he was thinking about quitting, but decided that could wait until tomorrow, when he'd made up his mind one way or the other.

But when the door opened and he turned around and saw Jennifer Blake, Fargo decided that he might just hire on with the devil himself if the job meant he'd be spending time with her.

6

Jennifer Blake sidestepped so she wouldn't be standing in the door, then paused to take in the room with her darting eyes, hazel with flecks of green. Those weren't bedroom eyes. They were doing the same thing he did when tracking: get the whole picture, complete to the smallest detail, into your memory, where you could work on it later if the need arose.

Fargo already knew all that he cared to know about what Kearny's telegraph office looked like, so he enjoyed this polite opportunity to examine Miss Blake.

She was a miss because no evidence of rings disturbed the smooth silk glove that covered the long fingers on her left hand. After filing that pleasing fact, Fargo grew more pleased as he continued his perusal.

The woman was taller than average—about five-foot-six, if he had to guess. She wore a pale straw hat, almost flat, held on by an embroidered chin strap. When she twisted her head to look at the far wall, he could see that most of her long cinnamon hair was bunned up behind the hat. When she turned his way again, she had a lean, expressive face. Her cheeks were almost hollow under high cheekbones, and her lips were thin, almost invisible as she set her mouth even tighter while she concentrated on memorizing the room and every man in it. Her age was hard to guess—twenty to twenty-five, somewhere in there.

Fargo didn't pay a whole lot of mind to what women wore, since they looked so much better without clothes. But Jennifer's outfit was memorable. Topside, a tan corduroy coat swelled agreeably in the right places. The coat's top three buttons were undone, revealing a pale linen shirtwaist. Just as the coat got serious about swelling for her hips, it stopped and a matching skirt took over.

She turned and again examined the room, her eyes locking on Fargo's. "You would be Mr. Skye Fargo?"

He tipped his hat slightly as he smiled. "I would. And you are Miss Jennifer Blake, I presume?"

She nodded. "May I speak to you in privacy?" She gave the rest of the room a look that implied she would be pleased if everybody else stepped outside for a few minutes.

They didn't, of course, so she stepped toward him, who offered her an elbow to hold as they went outside.

"How did you know who I was?" They were walking along the dusty path that led back to the parade ground in the center of the fort. She seemed intent on matching the Trailsman, stride for stride.

"I could ask why you were asking for me, but I already know," Fargo replied. He wasn't sure how much he should tell Jennifer, because when he'd hired on, Majors had wanted him to keep his job a secret. But then his last word from Majors had been to assist Jennifer in whatever she needed.

He compromised. "I'm out on an inspection tour of the Pony Express for Russell, Majors and Waddell. When I stopped here, there was a message waiting. Among other things, it advised me to assist you in whatever you were doing. That I don't know, but I do know that you're already something of a celebrity at Fort Kearny, at least in the telegraph office. Women aren't all that common on army posts."

She nodded. Then her voice got harder. "Drat that old Alex Majors. I wanted to do this all myself. I don't want or need a guide or a guardian. And then he assigns me one. Is there a chance you could ride on and proceed with your inspection, Mr. Fargo, and pretend that we somehow missed each other here?"

That wasn't at all what Fargo had in mind. At least, not until they'd gotten to know each other a little better. He'd had his bedroll to himself for the past fortnight.

"That depends, Miss Blake. I might be willing to go along with that if you explained just what it is you're doing. I just learned that part of my job is assisting you, and if it looks like I'd assist you best by being somewhere else, well, I'm willing to consider it. But I've got to have something to consider."

They were at the parade ground, where some troops were being reviewed in evening formation, although sunset was at least another hour away. Around its perimeter, off-duty officers and their wives or sweethearts strolled arm-in-arm. Fargo and Jennifer fit right in.

Jennifer hesitated before turning her eyes to meet his. "Perhaps I should tell you the whole story, Mr. Fargo."

"That's up to you."

"I want to be a reporter for the New York *Herald*, Mr. Fargo." She saw him blinking in wonderment. "What's wrong? Don't you think a woman can be a newspaper reporter?"

"You can do whatever you're of a mind to, as far as I'm concerned, miss." Fargo didn't bother to tell her she wasn't the first aspiring female reporter he'd met.

"I wish all men shared your enlightened attitude, Mr. Fargo. But the only one who will even give me a chance is that horrible Jamie Bennett at the *Herald*. And I have to earn that opportunity."

Fargo shrugged. "About all any of us ever get is a chance, Miss Blake. What happens after that is up to you, isn't it?"

She calmed a bit and quit gripping his forearm quite so hard. In fact, her fingers seemed to be exploring. "I suppose so. At any rate, I mustered up my courage and finally talked to Mr. James Gordon Bennett in his office. First I had to convince him that I had not come to his office because I wanted to be on the guest list for the next orgy on his yacht. But once I showed Mr. Bennett my clips—"

"Clips?" Fargo wondered aloud.

"Things I had written for other newspapers," she explained.

"I thought you said newspapers wouldn't hire women as reporters," Fargo interjected.

"They won't. But I had submitted stories by post, using a man's name for a pen name, of course, and those were accepted and published. So I showed those to Mr. Bennett, and he said they looked good. Then he said that if I could find a great exclusive story somewhere in America, and send it to the *Herald*, and he could use it, then he would throw tradition to the winds and hire me full-time."

Fargo looked up as the lieutenant in the square announced that the men, all slouching at attention in mismatched uniforms, were dismissed. The shadows were growing long, suppertime was near, and he and Jennifer were the only strollers left.

He turned back to Jennifer. "So your search for a big story brought you to Kearny, and you ran across Alex Majors somewhere along the way."

She nodded. "In New York, everyone is excited about the new Pony Express. People talk about it all the time. All the little boys want to be Pony Express riders when they grow up. But no correspondent has traversed the route and talked to the riders, to tell the entire story of a magnificent undertaking. If there's a great story in America, that's the story. And it's even more of a story if a woman writes it. At least that's what Mr. Bennett said."

"Sounds reasonable."

"I believed it would be best to get the cooperation of the owners of the Pony Express, so I talked to Mr. Majors in St. Joseph. He said it would be marvelous if the full story of the dashing Pony Express were told in New York, and he pledged his full cooperation."

"Which included me," Fargo muttered. His thoughts were on Majors. He certainly would like the biggest paper in New York to carry a glowing account of the dispatch and bravery of the Pony Express. It would get him more business and improve his credit rating on Wall Street. It might even get him out of his jam with Josiah Abernathy.

Fargo again felt a gnawing suspicion that he was somehow being used. But Jennifer was now walking so close that her hip occasionally swayed into his thigh, and he liked the way it felt. He might as well learn a little more.

"Mr. Majors said you were the finest scout, tracker, and wagon master in the business." Jennifer sounded sincere about that.

"And for years that same Mr. Majors would never hire me, even to shovel stalls," Fargo pointed out. "So I wouldn't take what he says too seriously."

Her voice perked up. "I can't imagine that. He was almost fulsome in his praise of your abilities. He said you were a better scout than Kit Carson, you tracked better than an Apache, you could get wagons from here to there faster and with less complication than any man alive. Maybe the great story is you, not the Pony Express."

Fargo instinctively pulled away from her a bit. "Wait a minute. If there's anything I don't need, it's having my name in a newspaper. I can find enough trouble without that. Let's just keep my name out of this."

Her eyes sparkled in her twilight nod. "Certainly. After all, I wanted to do this on my own. I believed it would make a great story: Educated City Woman Visits Wild West. And then Mr. Majors insisted that I find you, because he said it wouldn't do him or his company any good if harm came to me. So he told me to find you, that you were doing some sort of traveling inspection for him, and that you could be my escort to keep me out of harm's way."

"But I gather that you don't necessarily want to stay out of harm's way," Fargo muttered.

"That's true, Mr. Fargo." She pressed closer to him, so that her uncorseted right breast made its presence known to his upper arm. "And you don't want to be part of the story, so it appears to me that all things would work for the best if we were to pretend that we somehow missed each other here. Then you could go on your way and I could go on mine."

"Just what is your way? You're riding the Overland Stage and stopping at various stations where you have a chance to talk to the Pony Express riders?" She must have left St. Joe just days after he had and gotten ahead of him on the route while he had investigated to the north.

He knew she was nodding by the way her breast slid up and down his arm, and he silently ordered his stirring groin to quiet down and behave itself.

"Miss Blake, I don't know come here from sic 'em about writing for newspapers," Fargo explained. "So I suspect you know what would work best for you and what you want to do."

This talk with Jennifer Blake was going nowhere, despite how she was pressing against him. She'd already mentioned how much she prized her virtue. She was just a tease, used to getting what she wanted from men by batting her eyes and rubbing a little, then pulling back before things got interesting. That might work in the civilized East, but Fargo didn't care for her ways.

He wondered how close it was to seven, when he was supposed to catch a poker game with Ben Crenshaw.

"Excuse me a moment, Miss Blake." Fargo pulled all the formality he could muster into his voice. "I need to run over to the headquarters and see what time it is. I've got an appointment at seven."

She withdrew her hand from his arm. "Would you come back and escort me to my quarters?"

"Be proud to," he agreed. He turned and took off across the parade ground with a long lope that felt good after all that slow strolling.

The pendulum clock in the orderly room showed that twenty minutes remained until he was due at the poker game at the officers' club. Not plenty of time, but time enough to get Jennifer to wherever. He needed to eat, but certainly they'd be able to find a sandwich for him at the club.

Fargo legged it back to where he'd left Jennifer, in front of a low adobe barracks that was dark because it wasn't in use, either because the building was falling down and unsafe, or more likely because Kearny was undermanned these days, like every other western fort.

But Jennifer wasn't there. He called for her. Intense listening brought him no answer. Just the usual evening sounds of livestock, and distant frogs and crickets by the Platte River.

Like as not, Jennifer had decided to head for her quarters, wherever they were. Fargo didn't imagine she was apt to come to any harm on the parade ground of an active fort, so he started toward the officers' club, back behind the headquarters.

At his second step, he heard something muffled behind him, perhaps from the dark barracks. He halted in midstride and turned, raising one hand to his ear so any sounds from that direction would be amplified. The rustling and thumping were coming from inside the building.

Fargo trotted to the door and felt for its latch. It moved, but the door didn't, which meant it was barred. Which made it more than likely that the sounds had human origins.

Fargo edged over to a window. It was shuttered. As was the one on the other side of the door. He returned to the door and pressed his ear against it. Same sounds, only more distinct. He could discern gasps, heavy breathing, and a few masculine grunts.

He looked around, hoping a sentry might be nearby. Fargo would have preferred some official army permission for busting down a barracks door. But no one was near. He felt around the frame, hoping to discover some way of finessing the door. The door would be stouter than the crumbling adobe walls, so that argued against trying to ram it. Fargo pulled his knife. At shoulder height, he probed along the door's right edge with the knife. The blade met nothing, not even the usual wooden trim that served as a door stop—these barracks must have been drafty as tents in the winter.

After a few inches of probing, the far end of his blade met a heavy wooden bar. Fargo withdrew the knife a bit, so that only the point touched the bar, and traced an inch or two. Then he pushed the point in.

If he was lucky, this would be the kind of bar that sat atop two L-shaped brackets. Then he could just lift it off. If those brackets were D-shaped, so that the bar had to be slid in, rather than dropped in, then it would take half the night to work the bar out of the way.

The bar began to lift. Now it was just a question of how much brute strength Fargo could will into his hand, with the leverage working against him as he hoisted the bar with his knife tip. He wanted to hurry. What he could hear going on inside did not sound at all like a church social.

The idea was to lift the bar just enough on this side so that he could ease the door open and arrive without attracting attention, if possible. About the time his wrist muscles started tying themselves in knots, the bar moved back. It had cleared its bracket.

Hoping the hinges had been oiled recently, Fargo eased the door open enough for his arm to get through. He held the bar in his hand, to keep it from dropping with any telltale clatter. It still rested on the other bracket, so the door didn't swing open very far, but with some squeezing, he got his broad shoulders through and replaced the bar.

It was as black as strong coffee inside, and musty. Sounds came from the right, several rooms away. Fargo had to feel his way through the room, stepping slowly in the darkness. Navigating by sound, he prayed he wouldn't trip on anything.

The sounds got louder in the next room, and now he could make out whispers coming through the open doorway.

"Jesus, Willie, she's a hard one to hold still. Want I should hit her again?"

"Nah. I likes it when they wiggles some. Let's just get them damn bloomers down."

Fargo padded onward and discerned the situation from sound. The gasping had to be coming from a gagged Jennifer, who likely had a man standing behind her, holding her in place, likely with an arm crooked around her neck, so that if she struggled too much, the air supply down her long neck would get cut off. Willie was probably in front of her, peeling down her bloomers, no doubt with a pounding hard-on that would keep him from thinking clearly or noticing much that might be happening behind him.

Although Fargo now had a clear idea of who was where, throwing a knife was foolish in this darkness. He lengthened his stride and knew by the arrival of strong sweat and tobacco smells that he was within a yard of Willie, who was kneeling. His hands had to be working on Jennifer's bloomers.

Fargo cursed himself for leaving the woman alone, then atoned for his mistake. He pressed cold steel against Willie's neck. "Stand up, slow and easy," he ordered. "This has gone far enough."

Instead, Willie lunged forward to get away from the blade, while his partner shoved Jennifer into Fargo and started to bolt.

Fargo didn't want to stab Jennifer, so he sent the knife down. An anguished male howl split the night air, and warm sticky blood sprayed at Fargo's hand while he pulled the knife up. He momentarily wished for some turpentine to pour on the wound, but he had other concerns. The other partner in the attempted rape was either escaping or getting behind the Trailsman. Willie was screaming so loud that Fargo couldn't hear much else.

But he could sure feel it when Jennifer's knee connected with his shin. He supposed he couldn't blame her for being confused and kicking out at anything within range, but it still throbbed plenty as he leapt aside.

"Stay put, Jennifer," he shouted above Willie's tormented howl.

Since she was gagged, he couldn't tell what she mumbled. Fargo did hear hurried footsteps going toward the door.

He had replaced the bar, which would slow the man down for a moment. Fargo needed every instant of time he could glean to catch the man. The bar thudded to the floor, and the hinges screeched like angry owls as the door was jerked open.

Fargo raced after the escaping rapist and hoped there wasn't anything to stumble over. In seconds, he was at the door. Nobody was in sight, but he easily spotted the churned-up tracks of a running man and pounded after them, around the corner. Across an open field, twenty yards ahead, the man was trotting, taking it easy because his breath was coming in huge gasps.

"Stop right there," Fargo ordered.

Both these bastards had problems when it came to heeding him. This one did stop, but only to crouch and turn around with a pistol, whose muzzle flash erupted like fireworks.

Fargo didn't have time to duck. He leapt forward to gain ground, hollering on the way, as if he'd been wounded by a slug that hadn't come anywhere near him. That slowed the shooter, who was also momentarily blinded by his own muzzle flash.

Now Fargo was only four or five paces away. The crouched man leveled his pistol again, but the thrown knife had sliced into his heart before he could pull the trigger.

7

The next half-hour was a hectic whirl of flickering lanterns, shouting sentries, and inquiring officers. When the dust and confusion settled, the man in the field had been moved to the fort's morgue, a small room off the carpenter shop. Jennifer had a room at the post infirmary.

Down the hall from her, the victim of Fargo's unlit surgery was still screaming a lot, despite the gags in his mouth. Wounds to the testicles were painful. It seemed that the post surgeon didn't want to waste precious chloroform or morphine, although he seemed to enjoy pouring raw turpentine and grain alcohol on the screeching man's wound, "just to prevent septic contamination."

Fargo was soon comfortably sipping smooth officer whiskey and munching a ham sandwich. But his luck was down.

It was dealer's choice. Since Fargo was the dealer on this hand, he figured he'd give himself a fair chance, considering the miserable cards he'd been getting.

"High-low this time around," he announced. That meant the pot would be split between the high hand and the low hand. Any of Fargo's last three wretched hands would have taken half the chips under those rules.

But even that didn't work. After several rounds of dealing and checking, Fargo found himself showing a pair of treys, a pair of eights, and a six of hearts. His two hole cards were another trey and another six. He could go high with a full house, treys over eights, or go low with two pair, sixes and treys, with an eight on the side.

Making a decision was tough. His high hand wasn't any sure winner, and his low hand wasn't all that low. The other cards that showed didn't tell him anything he wanted to know.

But the essence of poker wasn't cards; it was reading your opponents. Unfortunately, Fargo didn't know any of these men well. Playing poker well demanded total concentration, just like following an Apache trail through slick-rock country. When they weren't cheating, professional gamblers earned every dollar they made. Many men could just relax and play the game for a little excitement and socializing, but that had never worked well for Fargo. Whatever he was doing, he got immersed in.

Tonight he was tired and had a lot on his mind, too much to give up unless he was faced with a life-and-death situation, which a poker game wasn't. He decided to go for the high hand with his full house, and chucked two more white chips in, to see Crenshaw's raise.

Captain Wesley Snyder, the fort's commander, sat at Fargo's left. Then came Second Lieutenant Obadiah Ross, the remount officer who ran the stable, followed by another second lieutenant, Dick Wilson, Snyder's aide-de-camp. Between Wilson and Crenshaw sat a first lieutenant, Ezekiel Sherman, an artillery officer in charge of the post's cannon crews.

Snyder saw the two chips and raised two more. Ross looked as indecisive as Fargo felt. He finally gulped and shrugged as he threw in four more chips to stay in the game.

Wilson grinned like that cat that just ate the canary, but he always grinned that way. The grin kept others from guessing his hand, and besides, he had good reason for the expression—his pile of chips was by far the largest. He was a damn good poker player. He also showed four hearts and a spade. If he had the right two that weren't showing, he'd be able to choose between a nothing hand and a flush, maybe even a straight flush, when the time came. He met the pot and then raised a red chip.

This was getting to be a more serious game than Fargo felt like playing, so he was relieved when there was knocking at the door of their private back room, followed by an announcement that the knocks were coming from Jacob Warren, the second lieutenant who had the duty watch tonight.

"Come on in, Mr. Warren," Captain Snyder ordered through his salt-and-pepper soup-strainer mustache. "I'm sure you wouldn't be bothering us if this weren't important." He sighed and laid his hole cards facedown.

"Captain, sir," Warren began, his pinpoint blue eyes flicking nervously around the table, pausing at Fargo. "We found some papers on those men."

"Any idea who they are yet?" The captain began to rise.

"Nobody knows yet. They appear to be drifters that wandered in. I sent some men around to ask questions."

Snyder's nod confirmed that that had been a good idea. "Hope they come up with something. Women ought to be safe inside a damn fort, and especially women who write for eastern newspapers that congressmen read." He pointed at Fargo. "I suspect that the gent Mr. Fargo here sliced won't be pushing himself at any ladies for a while, if ever. But has he said anything?"

"No, sir, not other than calling Doc Preston a lot of names I'd rather not repeat."

Snyder picked up his cards one more time and muttered before tossing them back down. "Looks like I'm out of this game." Fargo caught his come-along glance, leaned back, and joined him in leaving the game and walking over to the orderly room.

"I didn't hear all of your run-in with them, Fargo. You got any notion who or what those blackguards might have be?"

Fargo gave a shrug. "Black as sin when I met up with them. The one who lived was called Willie by the one who didn't. When there was some light, neither of them rang any bells. They had that drifter look—men who don't eat or bathe or shave on any kind of regular schedule."

"The sort you often find hanging around army posts," Snyder agreed. The captain pulled open the door to post headquarters and motioned for Fargo and Warren to precede him inside. Then he turned to Warren and asked about the papers.

A corporal made a face and held up one blood-soaked half-sheet. "Once it dries some, we might be able to read it. Guess whose pants pocket it was in?"

Fargo ignored his smile and asked if there were others.

"Found this one on the corpse. Feels like the same kind of paper, though it's hard to tell." He handed it to the captain, who peered at it without losing his puzzled expression, then passed it to Fargo without comment.

The half-sheet looked and felt like the good linen paper they used in bibles, except it was thicker. The few words had been scrawled by a pen with a fine metal nib. Fargo squinted at them before moving closer to a lamp.

"Replace Arkins, send to Box Elder. Decrease Consolidated Ophir with delay, results to me post-haste." The signature below looked like a crushed daddy longlegs, but it was likely somebody's initials.

"Think maybe they stole that somewhere, Fargo?" Snyder asked. "They didn't look the type to be carrying papers like that."

"Damn if I know what to think. Only thing on there that makes any sense is Box Elder, and that doesn't mean much of anything."

Snyder nodded. "Damn near every county has a Dry Creek, a Rock Creek, and a Box Elder Creek." He lifted his gray eyes to Fargo's. "You're welcome to that if you want to keep it. As far as I'm concerned, this matter's closed. But it may not be for you."

Fargo wondered just how much the captain knew about his plans for this trip, then decided that Snyder's caution had other grounds. If the dead man had kin somewhere, they might come after Fargo, and if the other man lived, he might not have any balls, but he'd sure as hell have ample reason for a grudge.

Moments later, a blood-spattered medical orderly appeared at the door with the announcement that despite the doctor's heroic efforts at preventing infection, the other man had just bled to death. His last words had just been some gritted swearing: no confession or even an explanation of who he was or what he'd been up to, besides the obvious rape attempt.

Then came a burly Sergeant Patrick O'Rourke. He stepped in, snapped off a salute to all present, and proclaimed that he was ready to report on his trip to nearby Dobytown. Snyder found a chair and told O'Rourke to go ahead.

"Those two had been in Dobytown for a couple days. All anybody knew them as was Willie and Sam. According to some barkeeps and the clerk at the hotel, they seemed to be edgy as long-tailed cats in a room full of rocking chairs, because they was waiting on something to arrive. A gent said he saw Willie get some mail this afternoon, just after the post stage come through." He caught his breath. "They got kicked out of the cathouse last night, on account of their surly ways and reluctance to spend more'n a dime to get laid, when everybody knows it's worth at least a quarter. And late this afternoon, they was talkin' about how they was in a hurry to ride west at sunup tomorrow."

"Good job, O'Rourke," Snyder complimented. He rose and beckoned Fargo back to his private office.

After the lamp and cigars were lit, Snyder pulled a jug out of a cabinet, filled two tin cups with bourbon, and invited Fargo to join him.

"Okay, Fargo, I know you're not out here just to drop by and say hi to Ben Crenshaw and sit in on a poker game. For one thing, you just got a message from Alex Majors to escort that lady reporter along the Pony Express route."

"I thought telegrams were private," Fargo said.

"They might be at a civilian telegraph office, but this is a military facility, and I'll be damned if I try to run it without knowing what's going on. You want to tell me, or do I have to figure out some way to hold you in the stockade for a spell, till your tongue loosens up?" He looked thoughtful. "Maybe for investigation into those killings? Or perhaps I could impress you into service as a scout. I can do that, you know, when the situation is threatening. The Sioux are fractious these days, and I'm shorthanded."

"I'd be cleared by any honest investigation," Fargo rejoined.

"True enough," Snyder conceded. "But it could take three or four months. You know how damnably slow government paperwork can be."

Fargo leaned back and explained the problem.

"Delayed dispatches." Snyder refilled his cup while Fargo waved aside the offer for more whiskey. "Somewhere along two thousand miles. Like finding one wave in the ocean. No wonder Majors wanted you to do it. And we do need Majors to stay in business. How in hell would we supply those western forts without his wagons?"

Fargo's insides started to churn when he thought about the flour on the wagons that would be arriving tomorrow at Kearny. He'd been feeling better, just being able to talk about what he was up to. Now this gut-clenching that came with just the notion of trying to be duplicitous again. Little wonder that he hadn't been playing poker well.

"Let me tell you something about a supply train that's coming in tomorrow," Fargo said.

"What about it? It's bound for Laramie if it's the one I know about that's due shortly. They're just stopping here for provisions and inspection."

"Well, if I was in charge of the inspection, I'd look at the flour wagons real carefully. Especially the sacks toward the bottom."

Snyder's bushy eyebrows lifted. "Thanks, Fargo. We'll do that." He stood and extended a hand. "Reckon we're close to even, now. You got a room, or can we find you one?"

Fargo took up Snyder's offer, and the next thing he really noticed was that he'd overslept, because the sun was well above the horizon. He checked on his supplies at the sutler's; they were packed and ready, whenever he wanted to pick them up, and Ben had already charged the stuff to Russell, Majors & Waddell.

He wasn't sure whether he was still working for them, especially when he saw the dust of the approaching supply train and a grim-faced inspection detail preparing for duty. But what the hell, he'd just given his word that he'd try to find the problem with dispatches. He hadn't promised that he'd help the company earn a few more nickels by foisting off tainted goods.

He was walking over to the stable to fetch his Ovaro when Jennifer called out from an open window at the post infirmary and motioned for him to come closer.

"Mr. Fargo, I can't thank you enough for coming to my rescue last night."

"You're all right, then? I'm sorry I left you by yourself. I never should have done that."

"No apology necessary, Mr. Fargo. They just stepped out of the dark. There was no way anybody could have seen them. And it's going to make such an exciting story."

"Wait just a minute, lady. You write whatever tale you want to, but keep my name out of it."

Glumness flashed across her face. "Mr. Fargo, you came to my rescue in the nick of time. How could I possibly ignore that in my dispatch to the *Herald*?"

Fargo considered breaking her fingers, then thought of bribing the telegraph clerk. Neither seemed sensible. He changed the subject. "Well, I'm riding out this morning. Now there's reason enough to suit Majors for you to go your way and me to go mine."

She bit her lower lip and gasped. "Mr. Fargo, after what just happened, how dare you leave me unescorted?"

"I have a job to do," he asserted.

"I'm part of that job," she insisted. "And I am free to leave at any time. I was not injured in that fracas. They just put me here for lack of a better place."

"So you've changed your mind?" Fargo had at least three hundred hard miles ahead of him. Even a willing woman would be a complication between here and Laramie. An ambitious tease would be pure torment.

"It's a woman's prerogative to change her mind. If I was assaulted here, right on an army post, how much more danger would I face if I were unescorted farther west?"

"A lot," Fargo blurted, annoyed. "Not just from white riffraff, but from Indians."

"Then you're agreed?"

Fargo grudgingly nodded. "Provided you abide by some rules. I'll explain those as we go along. Can you ride?"

She could.

Fargo borrowed a roan gelding from the army that more or less belonged at Fort Laramie and should be returned there someday, just to keep all accounts in order.

He had to give Jennifer credit for traveling light as they headed westward from Kearny along the Great Platte River Road.

"You mentioned rules, Mr. Fargo. What are they?"

"First thing is that we run on *my* schedule. I'll try to accommodate your work when we stop somewhere and give you time to talk to folks or whatever. And to write. But that isn't my main job out here."

"Just what is your main job, Mr. Fargo? You said it was an inspection, I believe."

"That's close enough. And that brings up something that bears repeating. You keep my name out of the tales you tell."

"Mr. Fargo, I could hardly do that. You're already an important part of my story of the heroes of the Pony Express."

"You can figure out a way, Miss Blake. Just to be sure, I might look over your work."

"That's censorship. That's illegal. We have freedom of the press in this country."

"Somewhere it must be written that I have a right to go about my life and my work without ending up in the damn newspapers."

"Suppose I talk to you about it whenever your name comes up?"

"Is that the best I'm going to get from you?"

Jennifer laughed. "Mr. Fargo, I don't want to cause you trouble. You're no man to trifle with. I'm most grateful for your timely assistance last night. But you said you had a job to do. So do I."

Fargo knew he'd feel better if her job involved returning to New York at this instant. But, hell, it sounded like she'd make an effort to get along, and if she could, so could he. He eased the Ovaro into a fast walk, much easier on the rider, and saw the next Pony Express stable, Platte Station.

It wasn't much more than a corral and several shacks. Nobody there looked capable of reading mail, let alone delaying it. They still had most of the day, so Fargo pressed onward past the stations of Craig and Seventeen Mile, hoping for Plum Creek by dark. They made it easily—her roan was a good horse—and Plum Creek's food, although greasy, was a king's feast compared to the stuff east of Kearny.

That was on account of fresh buffalo meat. "Was it a straggler or part of the southern herd?" Fargo asked the hostler, who had bragged on bringing the beast down, in the morning as they prepared to move on.

"Small bunch. I'd guess it was one of the leaders of the herd heading north."

"Can't blame the buffalo," Fargo agreed. "The grass is sweeter up there by this time in the summer."

"Yeah, but when all ten million of 'em start north, it's best to be somewhere else." Fargo liked the lanky kid who was tugging up Jennifer's cinch while she waited in the eating room. "That, and where there's buffalo, there's always Injuns. So I'd be watchful for Sioux to the west. They've been tolerable so far this summer, but you know how it is when they ride out, ready to shoot and bring somethin' back to camp. Sometimes a scalp suits 'em just as much as some fresh hump."

It was refreshing to indulge in trail talk for a change. Jennifer generally rode silently, staring wide-eyed at everything while occasionally jotting down some observation in a little hard-backed notebook she always carried. When she did speak, it was to ask questions about what something was called or why the trail took its swings toward and away from the river.

"Say," Fargo asked nonchalantly, "you know of anybody named Arkins who works one of these stations, on to the west?"

The kid looked thoughtful as he stepped back from the roan, his work done. "Was a Stick Arkins that worked in Julesburg a while back. Heard he got transferred after him and Black Jack Slade got in a set-to."

"Surprised there was enough of him left to transfer if he tangled with Slade."

"Wasn't much to start with."

"Suppose that's why he's called Stick," Fargo prodded, although he wouldn't have known Stick Arkins from any other rail-thin man.

"Reckon so," the youth agreed. "I know for a fact that the company transferred Slade. He was the boss of the whole central division, and now he's just runnin' a station at Horseshoe Creek. But you got to give the mean son of a bitch some credit. He did keep the wagons moving through his division. That guy they got in there now don't know shit from wild honey."

The conversation provided Fargo with two likely suspects. The current division manager might be causing the delays in some dispatches, just because he was inept. And as for Black Jack Slade, there wasn't anything that man wouldn't do if it caused trouble for others.

"This Black Jack Slade sounds like a colorful character," Jennifer remarked as they headed toward Willow Island Ranch.

"You could say that," Fargo agreed. "He's big, bigger than I am, got the homeliest wife in the known world, and he can be pleasant enough, though generally he's not."

"Just how unpleasant?"

The tale was a campfire staple along the Platte, but Jennifer obviously hadn't heard it before.

"Up ahead, the Platte forks. Though the trail in general follows the north fork, it swings down along the south for a ways, to a decent ford that used to be called the California Crossing. Nowadays it's Julesburg."

"Named after somebody named Jules?"

Fargo nodded. "Jules Reni, a Frenchman who used to run a little trading post there. When Russell, Majors and Waddell set up a route across there, Jules stayed on for a spell as the local agent. He was about as worthless as men get. He'd sell horses to folks bound west; then, that night, his men would go out and steal the horses back. Same for goods he sold."

"I hardly think the pious Mr. Majors would stand for such brigandry." Jennifer seemed more easygoing today, and she'd quit making doe eyes once she'd figured out that Fargo, unlike many men, would speak to her even if she didn't.

"Word did get back, after an inspection trip by Ben Ficklin, a lot like what I'm doing now. Ficklin hired Slade and told him to take care of Jules. Old Jules saw what was on Slade's mind, so he emptied a shotgun at him. Slade's friends hauled him off, close to dead, but he recovered.

"Meanwhile, Ficklin got wind of it and came back. He had Jules swinging off a cottonwood limb as his stage pulled out. But then some of Jules' outlaw buddies cut him down, just in time, and they went off and hid."

"This Mr. Reni sounds like a hard man to kill."

"He was," Fargo continued. "Slade recovered and found Jules at Pacific Springs. Knocked him down with a bullet in the thigh, then dragged Jules out and tied him to a corral post. Jules lived for two or three days out there while Slade used him for target practice—a knee or a shoulder every now and then."

Jennifer shuddered. "That's torture befitting the wild Indians. Didn't anybody try to stop Mr. Slade? Would you have if you'd been there, Mr. Fargo?"

"I don't know," Fargo confessed. "When you study on

Jules' career, the Frenchman wasn't getting anything he didn't deserve, and recall that he had tried to kill Slade."

"But now Jules Reni is gone."

"Not entirely. Slade cut off one of his ears and he uses it for a watch fob. He showed it to me once, when we were on speaking terms."

Jennifer gulped hard and lost her greenish cast as soon as she pulled out her notebook and started scribbling with a pencil stub.

8

Courthouse Rock, the first bit of interesting geography after better than a hundred miles of dreary sand hills, shimmered to the north through the dust and prairie haze.

Back in Julesburg, where the Pony Express forded the South Platte at the upper crossing, Fargo had learned that Stick Arkins now manned the station at Scott's Bluff. That was all the lead that Fargo had about the two men he had left dead at Kearny. They weren't his major concern anyway, since he didn't know of any way that the pair had been trying to delay Pony Express dispatches.

Since there was only one rider going each way each week, Fargo couldn't examine the procedure at each station. He'd seen an eastbound rider at Cottonwood Springs and a westbound yesterday at Lodgepole.

The station agent knew which day a rider was due, and had a horse ready to go. When the rider approached within a mile, he sounded the small horn they carried. The saddled horse was brought to the front.

Then the rider practically sat his horse down for a quick halt to the gallop. He jumped off. A stock tender grabbed the *mochila*, which sat atop the saddle, and flung it onto the new horse's saddle. A new rider followed, and moments later, he was pounding off into the distance. The whole process took no more than two minutes, and the letters inside the *mochila* were never touched, since the *mochilas* weren't opened.

This change to fresh horses happened every ten or twelve miles, so that the riders could push their mounts flat-out. One rider covered about fifty miles before a new one took over. Then he'd lay over until it was time to go the other way. Julesburg had been one of those layover stations, and Fargo had spent a whole day there, just so Jennifer could interview two real Pony Express riders and then send her story east via Pony Express.

The riders were all small and lean; Jennifer was bigger than most of them. Their diminutive size stood to reason; they really weren't anything more than long-haul jockeys. The lighter the rider, the faster a horse could go, and speed was the whole idea here.

Fargo didn't begrudge the time in Julesburg. It made him realize that his job would be simpler than he had first thought. Thanks to Jennifer's inquiries about how to get her precious prose to Manhattan as quickly as humanly possible, Fargo had learned that at these major stops where riders laid over, one pouch on the *mochila* was opened.

The other three pouches were sealed for the whole trip. But that one pouch was opened at every layover stop. Local dispatches were removed and outbound dispatches were added. That would provide a perfect opportunity to trifle with any dispatches in the *mochila*. Fargo figured to be on hand when the local express got sorted at the next place where riders laid over.

Jennifer looked over to him and asked if the spire, no bigger than a needle in the distance beyond substantial Courthouse Rock, was the famous Chimney Rock.

"I don't know what else it could be," Fargo conceded, "but it's awful hazy today to be sure of anything in the distance."

"It isn't always like this?"

"No. Usually you can see forever on the Great Plains. Not that there's anything to look at, but the air is clear."

"Why would it be hazy?"

"I'm wondering that myself. Could be a big fire off somewhere. They had a tremendous forest fire up in Canada a couple years ago, and there was haze clear down to Texas. That smoke'll wander all over hell and back."

She nodded, eyes closed as if she were trying to store Fargo's observation until she could write it down the next time she pulled out her little notebook. "What about the little cloud of dust up ahead?"

Fargo peered at it for a moment. It was long and hung low. "That's a wagon train. We can't see it because it's in a hollow. Looks like about two dozen wagons, from the size of it, although they aren't moving much, because the cloud is hardly stirring. Must be oxen. But even for that, they're just crawling along, barely moving."

"You can tell all that just by dust?"

He shrugged. "We'll be upon them within an hour. Then you can see for yourself whether I was right or not."

It was an emigrant train, and it had only twenty-two wagons, mostly canvas-topped Conestoga prairie schooners. They weren't in any hurry. Most wagons had only one yoke of oxen, instead of the customary two or three. The overburdened draft animals moved grudgingly, despite the pops of the whips. Their halting steps showed that they had sore feet.

Behind the caravan, a boy herded several horses and about a hundred head of plodding steers whose feet were even worse off—hooves worn down so much that their tender feet were bleeding. Fargo considered hailing the boy, but decided he'd talk to the leader first.

"Where's your captain?" he hailed at the first wagon he rode up to.

A whole family in tattered homespun was walking beside the wagon. Five kids, three of them boys, the oldest one maybe ten. A rawboned father whose boots were about to disintegrate, and a tiny mother who looked even more haggard. There was a youth, poking at the oxen, who had to be the man's younger brother, and the elderly couple looked to be the woman's parents, judging by their features. They were walking to lighten the load on the two straining steers, who were barely able to move the creaking wagon.

"Captain, what captain?" the walking man spat, looking envious that Fargo was on horseback and riding with an attractive young woman.

"What do you mean, 'What captain?' Every train has somebody bossing it."

The man nodded. "We did, till he up and vanished about a week out of Council Bluffs. 'Course, he got his money in advance."

Fargo had heard of such. Jennifer hadn't, so she was paying close attention so she could add another form of fraud to her tales of the trail.

"So who's running things now?" Fargo asked.

"Max Schottbein, up in the lead wagon. He's doin' his best, but somehow we got us a bunch of lame oxen, and it's still a long ways to Laramie."

"Thanks. I'll go talk to him, then."

With Jennifer riding at his side, Fargo proceeded toward the front of the plodding train, and found Schottbein. The tall blond man wasn't much more than twenty, and he walked with his wife, whose swollen bosom indicated that she was still nursing the baby she carried in her arms.

Fargo already knew what the train's problem was, but he wanted to know what was on Schottbein's mind. "Looks like you got slowed down," he greeted.

"That's a fact," Schottbein confirmed. "After we crossed

the South Platte, the country got rougher. Every cussed critter lost its shoes. They're sore-footed, a lot of them lamed. They're going to start dropping soon, I'm afraid."

"There's a way to fix that," Fargo began.

"Sure there is. Sure. Just have to shoe 'em again, right? But how the hell are we supposed to shoe 'em here?" He looked puzzled, as did Jennifer.

She broke in. "Skye, I've seen them shoe horses right out along the trail. They just build a fire, and the smith goes to work."

Fargo hated explaining the obvious, but maybe this wasn't all that obvious to her. "A horse will stand on three legs. An ox can't. He'll just fall over on his side, and they're a chore to get back up. They kick a lot, too, which makes shoeing them kind of dangerous."

Schottbein nodded. "At Council Bluffs, before we started, they had a sling that hung from a tree limb. Hoisted 'em up and then they were no trouble at all to shoe. But out here . . ."

His voice trailed off. The baby started to whimper, and Mrs. Schottbein decided to be demure about feeding it. She handed the baby to her husband, clambered aboard the wagon, then accepted the child and moved beneath the canvas.

There were trees up some of the higher draws, but they were just piñon, not big enough to hold an ox.

"You got a smith on this train?" Fargo inquired.

"No," Schottbein confessed. "There's a couple men that can put swell tires back onto wheels and replace fellies, that sort of thing, but they'd be the first to tell you they're just jacklegs when it comes to any real smithing, like forging ox shoes."

Since oxen had split hooves, each half took a shoe. That was double the work of making horseshoes, and it could take the better part of a day for an inexperienced smith to hammer shoes for just one ox—and they needed shoes for a hundred. Then there was the need to forge nails, along with the problem of actually putting the shoes on.

Fargo thought for a minute. This caravan had maybe another ten miles in it. Then it would halt for good, and a hundred people, mostly women and children, would be facing starvation and thirst, if the Sioux didn't show up first. It wouldn't take that long to get them moving again. "Think you folks could stand a big beef barbecue for dinner tonight?"

Schottbein smiled. "That I could. But what's your plan?"

"Get your wagons circled up at the next water, which is about two miles. Then put some men to work in the middle, digging a trench."

"Like a latrine trench?" Schottbein looked as puzzled as Jennifer. "Or is it for to barbecue meat?"

Fargo laughed. "Neither. Make it about a yard wide and maybe two feet deep. Smooth the sides as best you can."

"How long?"

"Long as possible. A hundred feet or better, if you've got room inside the circle."

Schottbein nodded. "Sure hope you know what you're doing, mister."

"I do," Fargo assured, although by their expressions, neither Jennifer nor the wagon leader would have bet money on it.

Still aboard the Ovaro, the Trailsman trotted past the train until he reached the herd of oxen who'd been taken out of service, since they were in even worse shape than those still attached to wagons. The drover, a good-natured red-haired kid who seemed to like his work, came over.

"You have something in mind, mister?" His eyes were mostly on Jennifer.

"That I do." Fargo waited for the boy's attention to

return to him. "One of us needs to cut out the worst-off critters, those that are apt to drop any minute now. The other can keep the others moving. Which do you want?"

"I already know which ones got feet worn down to the bone," the kid announced. "So maybe I should do the cutting."

"Fair enough," the Trailsman agreed. "I'll move the main herd. You cull them on the move, since we're hardly moving."

"What am I to do?" Jennifer asked, batting her eyes flirtatiously at the boy and swelling her chest provocatively. She was welcoming the opportunity to practice the teasing ways that Fargo ignored.

The boy stared at her appreciatively, then grew somber whenever he glanced back at Fargo.

"You can keep the culls bunched together while he goes back and forth."

"But I don't know how," Jennifer protested.

"Your horse does. Just let him do what comes natural to him, and you'll do fine."

Fargo didn't exactly hate trailing cattle, although there had to be better ways to spend time than in a cloud of choking dust and buzzing flies. He bunched the herd. With waves of his hat and some hollering, he got them to moving faster, although they protested.

Those that couldn't stand the pace fell back, blood streaming from the open sores at their feet. Back behind, the kid collected them into a bunch that Jennifer's horse was handling just fine. She looked perplexed, but held on gamely as the roan twisted and turned.

By the time they got to the circled wagons, there were a dozen stragglers.

From his wagon seat, Schottbein called out to the Trailsman. "The trench is almost dug. What now, mister?"

"Get me a few men with some goads. We'll send these

in, a few at a time. So get started on that. And I need some skinners."

"How many oxen will you slay for this feast?" Schottbein looked like a man who wished he'd never met the Trailsman.

Fargo realized he should explain. "The barbecue is just an afterthought," he shouted. "The hides are the main thing."

Jennifer caught up. "Hides? Don't the oxen need shoes?"

"Just what are your shoes made out of?" Fargo left her to figure that out and pulled out his Colt. It was better if he did this job, since the people who owned the dozen stragglers might have gotten attached to the beasts. He told the drover kid to make sure no oxen bolted, which was hardly likely, since the critters could barely walk, let alone run away. But it never hurt to be sure.

Five minutes later, they were all dead on the ground. Schottbein led four men, all toting short knives with wide blades and razor-sharp edges. Now was the time to finish explaining matters to Schottbein, who'd been more than cooperative, considering that a total stranger had just ridden up and started giving orders.

"Max, get those gutted fast, then skin them. As soon as you've got a couple hides, get somebody to slice them into squares about this big." Fargo indicated a one-foot square. "What's left, slice into strips like pigging strings that we can use for ties."

"You're going to shoe the other oxen with rawhide from the stragglers?" Max was catching on.

"That's the plan," Fargo confirmed.

"But how to reach their hooves?" Max wondered. "There's no way to lift them here."

"That's why we needed the trench."

Max looked puzzled, but Fargo let him stew and rode into the center of the circled wagons. About a dozen oxen stood alongside the trench, and better than twenty men looked even more confused than the oxen.

Fargo dismounted and collected four men. "Okay, gents, this is what we do." They followed him and his example. They goaded a steer to stand parallel to the trench. With surprising coordination for an impromptu crew, they shouldered against the steer's flank, and rolled it into the trench.

It protested with brays and snorts, lying on its back, feet sticking straight up into the air. But there wasn't a lot the animal could do about it, and so it stayed there, trembling.

"Now do that to the others until the trench is full. By then, we should have some shoes for them."

A few minutes later, he had to demonstrate how to tie a square of leather around an ox's sore hoof so it wouldn't fall off. The men caught on quickly enough; their lives depended on doing this well and quickly.

Then one husky wife had cornered him. "I'm Loretta Carson. Who are you?"

"Skye Fargo, ma'am. Anything else you want to know?"

"Indeed there is," she announced before he had a chance to turn and go get some more hide squares and tie strings. "I wanted to thank you for sharing your knowledge. I suggested the same thing to Mr. Carson, but he wouldn't listen. I thought if we could wear leather shoes, so could our steers. He said I didn't know anything."

"Some men are like that," Fargo conceded, eager to get on with the work. This stalled wagon train was a sitting duck, and the sooner it was ready to move again, the better.

"Mr. Fargo, I know we can roast an oxen or two this evening. But it would be shameful to leave good meat to waste." She said it with the force of someone who'd gone hungry a time or two and didn't ever want that to happen again if there was any way to avoid it.

"Indeed, it would be a shame to waste good meat, Mrs. Carson—" Fargo was interrupted by a shout from outside the circle.

"Injuns. Everybody inside and grab your rifles."

Fargo instantly turned and leapt up to a wagon seat for a better view. Five mounted Sioux braves stood on a ridge about a mile away. He stared closely. If they were just the vanguard for others, then they would be waving their lances and shields, to signal the rest of the party that this was a good day to raid, plunder, and maybe die.

But they weren't signaling, and when he studied their unadorned lances and noticed that they weren't toting coup sticks, he realized that this was just a hunting party, not a war party.

That didn't mean that the Oglalla Sioux wouldn't get in a fight today, but that hadn't been their intention.

Fargo did not want them to change their minds. He stepped out a bit, so they could see him more clearly, and began to gesture. Sign language was perfect for this kind of communication. He asked for a parley with their leader, midway between them. Then he found Schottbein. "Max, I'm going to go talk to those Indians."

"You want us to cover you?"

"No," Fargo said. "It may come to where we need weapons. But for now tell every man here to put guns inside his wagon, and to be standing clear. The last goddamn thing I need while I'm in a parley is for some hothead to start shooting back here."

Schottbein nodded. "I can see why. It won't be easy, though."

"It's about our only chance. There's just the five of them. But if they don't come back or if a fight starts, then tomorrow there'll be five hundred of them. I can ride off and outrun them. You can't."

Fargo looked around for Jennifer and saw her flirting with the half a dozen men who were rolling the shod oxen over and standing them up. Fortunately, they were all trying to impress her by each working harder than the next, so Fargo decided to leave well enough alone. If her coquettish teasing helped, then she might as well do what she was good at.

The pinto seemed wary of approaching the brave on the spotted pony. After the introductions, it turned out they both knew each other by reputation, although not personally. Makhpiya-Luta, better known as Red Cloud, was reputedly the fiercest warrior in the Oglalla band. But as he pointed out, he was not wearing war paint today.

"We just ride to see if the buffalo have come close yet from the south," he gestured. "The dimness in the air means that the big herd is drawing near."

That explained the prairie haze. Several million moving hooves could produce plenty of dust. "Some leaders have passed, I have been told," Fargo responded. "It was a white eyes who said that, but I think he was telling the truth, even though that comes hard for a white eyes."

Red Cloud laughed. "We found some leaders, too." Then he glanced at the train. "But that was not enough, and our people have great hunger."

He was hinting that with all that fresh beef down there, the emigrants ought to share. It wasn't just sharing. Way back when, if, say, a Kiowa band was crossing Oglalla hunting grounds, the Kiowa would give presents to the Sioux. It was sort of like using a toll road.

The Indians expected the whites to extend the same courtesy.

Fargo had accepted it, but a lot of whites just saw it as begging or worse. He explained that they had had to kill some oxen. Two would be roasted tonight. Red Cloud's band was welcome to the other beef, within reason.

"Nothing that still walks?" the warrior asked. Indians always preferred beef on the hoof. It stayed fresh that way, and it carried itself, no small consideration when everything you owned had to travel by horseback.

"None of those could walk to your lodges." Fargo explained their sore feet. "But after you and your men ate your fill, you could cut and dry some of the other meat, then take it back to your helpless ones. That should get them by until the big herd comes."

Red Cloud nodded and waved for the others to join him.

"Wait until I can wave you in," Fargo interrupted. "It's going to take some explaining. Many will be afraid to have you in our camp."

Dealing with Red Cloud was easy compared to explaining matters to the folks on the wagon train. "I want no guns out," Fargo ordered the assembled crowd. "If you want to stay in your wagons, that's fine. But if you deal with these Indians, be friendly about it. All they want right now is food, not a fight. But they'll give us more fight than we can handle if we start one."

A few of the men grumbled, but most were tired enough to want to avoid anything as taxing as a fight.

Upon their arrival, the first thing the Indians did was gorge themselves on the offal from the butchering. They preferred organ meat.

Fargo declined Red Cloud's generous offer to share, but stayed close by. Notebook in hand, Jennifer joined him.

"Maybe you'd better get in a wagon, honey," he advised.

"Not on your life," she insisted, eyes flitting from pencil to feasting Oglalla, so she could capture the scene. "I never imagined there would be a day as interesting as this one. A stalled wagon train saved by your knowledge. The oxen looked so comical on their backs. And then Indians—and they're not at all hostile."

"Don't fool yourself," Fargo grunted. "They can get plenty hostile. But I hope you do write this. People ought to realize somehow that Indians are just that, Indians. They aren't noble savages and they aren't blood-thirsty barbarians, either. But it seems like everything I've ever read about Indians made them one or the other."

"Then what are they?" Jennifer pushed.

"Just people trying to get by in a mean place. Which means they've got to be mean to survive. Anybody that stays on the Great Plains has to be rough. It's that kind of country."

She nodded. "That's the first time I've heard it put that way, Skye, and I believe you're right. The white plainsmen you mentioned, like Jack Slade or Jules Reni, are just as savage. A harsh land demands harsh people."

By now, Red Cloud was almost treating Fargo like an old friend when he stood up, blood trails running down from his mouth to smear his entire bare chest and most of his breechcloth. "We will cut up for drying what we can carry on our horses to the helpless ones," he gestured. "But there will be much left."

Before replying, Fargo turned to Jennifer. "Go back into the wagons and get Mrs. Carson and whoever she gossips with. She's the one that was worrying about meat going to waste."

Jennifer looked perplexed, but didn't argue before scurrying off. She returned a few minutes later, Mrs. Carson and four other middle-aged women in tow.

The Sioux looked as apprehensive about the women as the women did about them until Fargo explained his plan.

Red Cloud smiled before replying. "Pale women are so lazy. They make their men do much work, so white eyes cannot live like true men, who hunt and fight. Are you certain these women will work?"

Mrs. Carson had been pretty worked up about wasting meat, so Fargo felt fairly confident. He nodded.

"Then we will be pleased to show the pale women how to slice the beef into thin strips and dry it with the sun, so they will have food for their helpless ones."

Fargo had the feeling that Red Cloud included all palefaced men in the "helpless ones" category, but he let that slide. He explained matters to Mrs. Carson. She made a face, but she stepped over to Red Cloud and knelt beside him and a pile of fresh-skinned beef.

After a short demonstration and some explanations that Fargo had to translate, she had the rest of her sewing circle hard at work. When the train rolled out tomorrow, it would have oxen that were able to work and at least a week's supply of meat pinned to the canvas as it dried. Hell, if the women had some spices, Fargo might even show them how to make jerky before riding on.

Besides, he gathered that one of the younger women, a saucy little brunette, had just been widowed, and he decided to try consoling her tonight. Win or lose, that had to be an improvement on another night of sleeping solo just a yard or two away from warm-eyed but cold-shouldered Jennifer.

9

As it turned out, the pert young widow—she couldn't have been much over eighteen—had considerable need for consolation. When something disturbed his satisfied sleep, Fargo blinked groggily and glanced upward out of habit. A few puffy clouds floated in the direction he faced, but he could tell that dawn would be coming soon because the Big Dipper was sitting right under the polestar.

Much closer, and much more interested in the pole Skye brandished right beside her, the young widow finished murmuring something tender into his ear and rolled atop him. While she presented a growing nipple to his mouth, her smooth knees wriggled around his shaft.

His hands instinctively felt their way to her soft but muscular rump, which was bobbing and sliding. He pressed and caressed, a silken cheek in each palm. That inspired her to demonstrate just how ready she was by rolling her moist and open slit around his navel.

Since this was their fourth go-round since bedding down, Fargo wasn't in any hurry. All the built-up frustration of traveling with reticent Jennifer had erupted the first two times, when Beth had been just as eager to cure her month of loneliness. The third time, along about midnight, had been long and leisurely, comfortable and relaxing.

Within a couple minutes, Fargo's attention began to stir down there by her knees. Beth slid back and clamped his upright shaft high between her side-swiping thighs. "I never tried this before." She giggled. "It feels funny."

Fargo wished there was more than just a sliver of a moon, so he could improve his view of Beth. Especially when she slid back a little more and rose onto her knees before easing down to take just the tip of his pulsing organ.

Even in the faint light, though, Fargo could see enough to enjoy the view. Beth, her long dark hair let down so that curls tumbled over both shoulders, had her head back, and a wicked smile. Her ample breasts bounced delicately, in keeping with the slow rhythm they were establishing. He'd thrust up, and so would she, only not quite as much.

He was gaining only a fraction of an inch with such minute strokes, but this was one occasion when he didn't mind taking his time. His long arms enabled his hands to explore her thighs, breasts, and bottom, while his eyes feasted on the spectacle.

"Oh, Skye, this is marvelous," she gasped while bobbing on his pole like one of those painted wooden horses on a merry-go-round. Fargo couldn't help but twist his head, just to see whether Jennifer, who was sleeping about twenty yards away, had been awakened by Beth's announcements, which were getting louder with every thrust. But so far, Jennifer seemed to be sleeping soundly.

"I see stars," Beth proclaimed, and it sounded loud enough to carry to those stars. "And flashes in the sky."

When her head tossed forward on her next bounce, Fargo checked. Her eyelids were batting a lot, so maybe all those flashes and stars were her own doing, with some help from his inspiration that she kept sliding farther down.

He returned his attention to thrusting upward, pushing inward to fulfill an insistent desire that was starting to throb through every part of his body.

Beth let loose. Her body came down just as fast as her voice rose. "Oh, God, more. That's all for me," she hollered.

Fargo began to tremble all over as he exploded deep within her. Fluttering like a leaf in a storm, Beth pitched forward to grab Fargo's shoulders as she rocked back and forth and up and down and any other possible direction that would allow her to get a little more of him inside her.

"The whole world is shaking," she shouted as Fargo pumped his final outburst into her. "Glory and hallelujah!"

They settled down after that as she clutched forward to press her body against his while they were still locked together. Fargo eased back against his blankets.

His first thought was that this had been one marvelous evening. Then he realized that the earth really was shaking with a low, steady vibration. And what sounded like a purring woman was in fact a distant rumble.

It wasn't a storm, because the clouds were still flitting in the sky to the north. But Beth had been looking south a minute ago.

"Beth, honey, did you really see flashes?" Fargo asked smoothly.

"Oh, of course," she sighed. "Dozens."

Fargo's deepest wish was that he was wrong. But that damn rumble was getting louder, and he knew for damn sure that no matter how much pleasure he had with a woman, the ground never really shook. Yet it was vibrating enough to jingle some of the wagon traces.

"Get up and dressed," he ordered Beth.

"You're not worried that somebody will find us, are you, honey? Pooh, I don't care what those old biddies think."

"I don't either. But you'd better get inside your wagon, fast as you can."

"Why?"

Fargo rolled her to his side, then stood up and began pulling on his balbriggans. "Because there's a goddamn buffalo stampede on its way."

"You're sure it's coming this way?"

For every bit of pleasure he'd just enjoyed with Beth, he was now gaining a corresponding amount of exasperation. "No, I'm not. I can't see enough to tell. But I know there's a buffalo herd to the south, and I know that it's stampeding, and it's getting louder and the ground is shaking more every second. So they're coming this way."

He paused, then pointed at Jennifer. "And get her up and into your wagon, too, fast as you can. I don't know how much time we've got."

"Should I rouse the camp?"

"Yeah, some of it. Those that are sleeping out, make sure they get inside wagons. Get Jennifer to help."

After some hurried dressing, Fargo climbed onto a wagon seat, the highest perch available, and tried to see what was happening.

The sounds were clearer up here. The herd was definitely to the south, and perhaps five miles away, where the Platte River ran. Buffalo generally didn't stampede, but all those shooting stars that Beth had seen could have spooked the migrating herd, which numbered in the hundreds of thousands. Maybe they'd stop at the river, but Fargo wasn't willing to bet his life, or anyone else's, on that proposition.

He scanned the camp as he heard Beth rousing Jennifer. The wagons were drawn up in a circle. Since the open prairie air, when the weather was good, was more pleasant than the stifling interior of a wagon, most people had spread their bedrolls outside. Many were under the wagons, though, and Fargo smiled as he noticed some telltale heaving and humping under some blankets on the far side.

After their shoeing, the oxen had been driven down to

the river for water, then herded back to a nearby hollow. Along with the few horses, they would have to be driven into the center of the wagon circle, or else all the live-stock would be lost in the stampede.

After grabbing his saddle and tack, Fargo took long and rapid steps toward the oxen. He didn't dare run, which meant too big a chance of dropping a foot down a prairie-dog hole and finding himself on the ground when thousands of sharp hooves were headed his way.

The distance seemed longer than the quarter-mile he remembered, and he didn't have to worry about waking the cattle. They were lowing and milling, and the drover kid was saddling his own horse when Fargo arrived.

"Something's sure spooked these critters," he explained as he pulled the cinch, then kicked the horse's inflated belly to let the air out, and tugged some more to be sure his saddle would stay on.

"Buffalo stampede," Fargo explained, saddling the Ovaro. "We need to run these oxen into the wagon ring. I'll go make an opening, and you start moving them. I'll be back to help as soon as I can."

The kid would have his hands full, but it wouldn't be much use for him to get the cattle moved if the place wasn't ready for them. And the folks sleeping in the wagon circle wouldn't find ox hooves, even in makeshift leather boots, any improvement on being pummeled by buffalo hooves.

Fargo urged his big pinto back to the wagons. To the east, the first gray fingers of dawn poked into the sky. To the south, the prairie itself appeared to be in motion, a boiling dark sea, and the noise was like pounding surf.

Most men were helping their families into their wagons, although one old-timer was cussing Jennifer hard for disturbing his sleep, and some others, apparently done loading their wives and children, were standing around, yawning and looking for something to do. They wouldn't feel right if they just huddled in some shelter.

"Pull this wagon out," Fargo commanded from outside, "so we can drive the stock in."

Eight men immediately ran over and put their shoulders to it.

Fargo sorely wished for some hot coffee to sharpen his wits after a night with Beth that had involved a lot more passion than sleep, but it would be a while before any fires got built today. The incessant and rising drone of the approaching herd pounded at his ears.

Meanwhile, the oxen milled, so they weren't making much progress toward the wagons. He thought to rebuke the drover for letting that happen, then realized that it was the only way a lone drover had any hope of controlling the spooked animals. All one man could do by himself was make them go round in circles and then nudge them toward where he wanted them to go. Fargo's estimation of the kid rose considerably by the time he got next to him.

"You point and flank them, and I'll ride drag."

The kid nodded, and even in the dust and dimness, his smile showed. Grown men never volunteered to ride drag when there was a kid around for that dusty and tedious chore.

But Fargo had figured the kid, who tended these animals every night, would know more than he did about handling this particular herd.

He was right. The young drover pushed his wiry mustang into the herd, which instantly halted most of the milling. With some nudges, he got his mount close by the lead ox, the one that wore a tinkling bell. Moments later, the kid had a lasso around the animal's horns, and he and his horse were tugging the leader from the center to the fore.

With their natural leader out front, the oxen straightened out, although they were still jumpy during the short drive. So was Fargo. He almost welcomed it when a steer bolted out of line, so he could go shoo it back and think about that, rather than how much louder the roar was getting.

How far were the buffalo now? Two miles maybe, which meant perhaps fifteen or twenty minutes before the thundering herd arrived. Now there was no question that the wagon train was in their way. The leading edge of the buffalo herd stretched east and west for as far as Fargo cared to look. Fargo thought of sending a few shots from the Sharps down that way, but dismissed the notion. It was more likely to rile the herd than to scare it off.

Once the buffalo arrived, he had his doubts about whether even the stout Conestogas would be able to stand up to the pressure. The wagons would be buffeted by tons of moving, angry muscle. Fargo had seen even big Murphy wagons tip over in such tumults, their stout oak beams nothing more than slivers and kindling after the buffalo had passed.

But the wagons were the only shelter they had, so they'd have to use them, no matter how flimsy they might be in the face of what was coming. Fargo let loose a few oaths, then wished again for some hot coffee, right off the campfire.

Fire. No hope of starting anything big enough to turn the approaching herd, but a blaze on the south side might annoy the buffalo enough so that they'd veer around it, like water in a river flowing around an island. A fire might not work, but it sure couldn't hurt.

Fargo reined up the Ovaro as the last steers trotted into the circle. Jennifer was even helping by holding the tongue up as the men shoved the gate wagon back into place. "Grab some fuel," Fargo hollered, "and bring it to me. Pronto."

He wanted some coal oil, but realized he'd just have to make do for kindling. He rode out about a hundred yards, to where the buffalo grass was withered. He dismounted and knelt, grabbing clumps of the grass and throwing it into a tiny heap.

When he looked up, he realized he had about five minutes before he'd have to rush back. Otherwise, he'd get stomped into jelly. He glanced back and saw frightened men carrying gunnysacks of buffalo chips, the cordwood of the Great Plains. A few had armloads of piñon limbs or cottonwood branches that they'd collected somewhere else.

Fargo built a knee-high tepee out of the dried grass and struck a lucifer. The matchstick flamed just fine, but it might as well have been a block of ice for all the effect it had on the grass, which didn't even bother to smoke or crackle.

A man arrived bearing cottonwood branches and wordlessly handed Fargo a chunk that still had bark. Fargo popped off the loose, rough bark and shoved it into the center of his grass cone. The inside of cottonwood bark was stringy and generally provided easy kindling. It smoked and hissed a bit, but refused to spread the flame of his match.

"Shit and double shit," Fargo swore. He had time for one more try. The men had dumped their fuel around him, and then demonstrated their good sense by hightailing it back to the shelter of their wagons. He didn't blame them a bit.

He knew the stuff would catch fire if he could just get some tinder to catch. He heard something at his side and saw Jennifer kneeling next to him.

"Get your ass back in those wagons, honey," he grunted. He reached over to reinforce the message. His hand brushed against his shirt pocket, and he heard something rustle.

Paper. Paper was the next best thing to coal oil for starting fires. He jerked it out. The blood-soaked half-sheet from the man who had bled to death in the Kearny infirmary was now pink-tinged and dry as a popcorn fart. He unfolded it and started to shove it atop the cotton-wood bark when Jennifer stayed his hand, then grabbed the sheet.

"No, don't use that," she gasped. "You can see the writing now. It might be important."

"So is staying alive, lady. Get your ass back to those wagons and let me worry about how fires get started."

"No, Skye, don't," she protested. She pulled her own precious notebook out of her pocket and ripped out three sheets. Two she dropped before Fargo, and the third she wadded and tossed in.

Fargo wadded the other two. The ground was pounding like the foundation of a stamp mill, and the gamey smell of buffalo hide was overwhelming. He looked up to see the leading edge only three hundred yards away, and closing fast.

He tossed in the match and hoped Jennifer had enough sense to already be aboard the Ovaro. She had. He vaulted aboard an instant later, her rump rubbing against his crotch as he kicked the Ovaro toward the wagons.

The fire had been a foolish notion anyway. There wasn't any hope that it would have time to amount to more than a few puffs of smoke before the herd trampled it into oblivion. The major worry now was getting into the wagons somehow, and they had been circled pretty tight. There certainly wasn't any way that the Ovaro, being ridden double, would be able to outrun the buffalo for more than a couple miles.

The big pinto didn't want to gallop straight into the wall of wagons. But the horse veered a little to the right, found an opening, and steeplechased its way over the tongue. There was enough clearance for the horse, although one of Fargo's kneecaps tried to take a dashboard along.

They landed amid swirling oxen. The ox beneath them kicked up at the big pinto across its back. The horse reared. Fargo found himself landing hard on his ass. He didn't even have time to catch his breath before a steer stomped on his other knee. Despite all that talk about soreness, the shod hoof didn't feel one bit tender to him as it hammered his kneecap.

Clutching a neck, Fargo got to his feet, realized that wouldn't be enough, and rolled aboard an ox back.

The steer didn't seem to mind, and Fargo got his bearings. Jennifer, with a saddle horn to clutch, had stayed atop the Ovaro, which had taken her over to a wagon. A man was helping her get off the horse and inside the canvas.

Fargo looked back the way he had come, half-expecting to see buffalo leaping through the same gap. Though the entire world was shaking furiously with so much noise that it sounded as though the earth was falling apart, he only saw a few buffalo.

Mostly there was a cloud. He nudged the steer that way and saw that his hasty fire must be doing some good. It was smoking a lot, and it looked like the buffalo were generally dodging it.

Fargo wanted to know exactly what was happening. So he slid from one ox to the next until he was able to pull himself into a wagon seat.

By now, his fire had had a chance to spread into the buffalo chips. The crackling flames weren't high, but they produced a prodigious quantity of acrid ocher smoke. The herd split at the smoke.

A few buffalo had wandered into the area between the fire and the wagons, but they were too upset and confused to be a real worry. Shouted chatter was moving from wagon to wagon, and Fargo quickly learned that the wagons on the north and south had both been bumped hard a few times, but nothing serious.

For the first twenty minutes or so, a buffalo stampede was a most impressive spectacle. But it was like watching a big river flow by. It all looked much the same after a while. The dust was thick and the smoke got in the way, but even when a vagrant breeze cleared the sky some, Fargo could see no end to the herd. The far bank of the Platte, better than five miles distant, was a solid wriggling mass of close-packed brown fur.

Fargo knew he'd watched it long enough when his knees reminded him that they'd been banged. He crawled inside the wagon.

There was a plain-faced woman in homespun, at least two frightened kids curled up and trying to sleep under a blanket, and a rather chubby curly-haired man in bib overalls. The other occupant was Jennifer, who had her notebook and pencil out.

"Oh, Skye, let me introduce you to Homer and Peggy Jennings. They're from Ohio, bound for California. I was just asking them about their trip."

Fargo sagged against a chest before tipping his hat and grunting that he was pleased to make their acquaintance. He started to apologize, but before he could try making amends for his rudeness, he was snoring.

When he awoke, he was in an empty wagon. It was near sundown, and the usual evening activities were under way. Cookfires were being kindled, dough was being kneaded for dutch ovens, kids were running around and hollering like wild Indians, and one busybody was cackling as she pointedly commented on the way that Beth the widow had slept through the day's excitement.

Fargo didn't see fit to enlighten her. She did tell him that the last of the herd had passed about an hour ago. His nose told him where to find some coffee, over toward the other side. He found Jennifer there. She sidled over to give him room on the log she sat on, an invitation for him to join her.

"It's going to be a great story," she announced.

"What? A bunch of scared animals running by. That's the whole story."

She smirked and began to read from her notebook. "Today I saw an entire emigrant train—twenty-four men, twenty-six women, seventy-three children—saved again by the courage, tenacity, and ingenuity of one man who happened by at a fortuitous time."

Fargo wanted to stop her right there, but he had a mouth full of coffee. And he was savoring it too much to feel like dropping the cup so he could choke her.

"I say 'saved again' because yesterday he found the wagon train barely able to move, isolated in the barren land of the savage Dakota Indians of Nebraska Territory. The rough rock-strewn prairie had lamed the oxen after wearing away their metal shoes. Only he knew of a method that would allow the poor beasts to walk again and resume their burdens."

"Enough," Fargo protested.

"Don't you want to hear about how you kept the Indians from attacking? And how you saved the train from a buffalo stampede?"

"Didn't we have a deal that you'd keep my name out of whatever you wrote? Or does your word mean anything?"

Jennifer laughed lightly as she laid the notebook down. "You should listen more closely, Skye. I didn't use your name, did I?"

"Guess not," Fargo conceded. "So you're going to post that as soon as you can, and everybody that reads the *Herald* can wonder who this mysterious hero is? They'll think you're making it up."

"That's why I'd like to use your name, Skye. The story would be more credible then. Maybe I'll be able to persuade you to change your mind before I send in my dispatch."

"Wouldn't bet on it." He drained his tin cup and leaned forward to pour some more.

"I bet you would if I acted like Beth," she whispered. "That wanton hussy."

Fargo turned and glared at her. "What Beth does is her business, not yours. And what I do is my business, not yours. You've got no call for saying anything."

Jennifer reddened. "I'm sorry. It's just that, well, I've tried to reason with you."

"No, you've tried to flirt with me. That might work with schoolboys and it might work with Mr. James Gordon Bennett, but it's not something I care to put up with."

She shrugged, then seemed to recall something that made her brighten. "Mr. Fargo, do you recall the paper you had planned to use for kindling the fire?"

Fargo nodded. "Sure. What about it?"

She pulled it out of a coat pocket and handed it to him.

Rec'd word Majors may disrupt plan with special secret agent—big man but lean, long black hair, and full beard, blue eyes. Rides a pinto stallion. Dispatch him.

The signature was the same spider squash as on the other sheet that had come from the other man, the paper that had revealed Arkins' name.

Fargo lifted his eyes and met Jennifer's. "I don't think they were talking about putting this man on the Pony Express when they said to dispatch him."

"No," she agreed. "And I think the man they're talking about is you."

Fargo couldn't deny that. The two unknown drifters had been at Kearny for several reasons, and killing him was one of them. "A man gathers enemies," he commented.

"You picked one big enemy," Jennifer announced. "Look at that signature."

Fargo examined the inked scrawl again and still couldn't make out any pattern that made sense. "What, somebody that doesn't know to sign his own name?"

"I've seen it before, and I would know that signature anywhere, Skye. It had to come from the pen of the richest and most powerful man in America, Josiah Abernathy."

10

All the dust and confusion of the emigrant train lay a day behind them. After a night at Mud Springs, where Jennifer slept on the kitchen floor and Fargo in the dugout where the horses also took shelter, they rose early and pressed on. The sun was barely up when they passed Courthouse Rock and its smaller neighbor, Jailhouse Rock. A few miles later came Chimney Rock, which looked like an inverted funnel; its sheer spire rose more than three hundred feet from the base. Ahead loomed Scott's Bluffs.

The sheer main bluff rose seven hundred feet. It extended almost to the North Platte River, with impassable chopped-up badlands dropping from its elevated base to the river. To its left was an even larger eminence, the South Bluff, a marl escarpment that went south for several miles to join the rough Wildcat Hills, which flanked the river on this side.

Between the two out-of-place mountains was a narrow V-shaped gap whose bottom was perhaps three hundred feet below the summits it pierced. One well-used road headed straight for that gap; at a fork just ahead, another road veered to the left for another tortuous route through this gateway to even rougher country farther west.

"How will those poor emigrants get through there without a good captain?" Jennifer asked, her eyes gulping in the first real scenery after a fortnight of bleak sand hills.

"They won't have any trouble finding the route. So many wagons have gone through here for so long that they've worn ruts in the rocks up ahead. Not just ruts. It's more like a ditch that's a yard deep and a wagon wide."

Jennifer sounded relieved. "So they'll get through all right?"

Fargo shook his head. "They really do need a guide. Schottbein does his best, but he doesn't know the country. They could save a lot of time up there if they knew where to double up on the upgrades, where to chain their wheels going down, that kind of thing."

"Too bad you can't do it, Skye."

Fargo didn't miss anything about the emigrant train except Beth the lonesome widow. But he kept that to himself. "Chances are somebody will be hanging around at one of the stage stops up here that could help them through, maybe hire on for the rest of their trip. I'll see if I can recruit some help for them."

He didn't feel nearly as excited as Jennifer. She was marveling at the landscape that rose around them, and he was looking at what was close by. Scores of graves pocked the ground beside the trail here. Cholera, pneumonia, Indians, pleurisy, exhaustion, starvation, childbirth complications, firearms accidents, kids crushed under wagon wheels. Every imaginable way to die was represented.

The east approach to the gap through Scott's Bluffs resembled one long churchyard. The bluffs themselves were tombstones of a sort, their very name a memorial to Hiram Scott, a fur trapper who had crawled here to die twenty years ago after his companions had abandoned him.

Fargo hated the place. Not for its dismal history, but because he had often been a wagon master on this route.

Getting heavy wagons up and over the narrow, steep road through the bluffs was generally two days of tedious work, and no matter how careful you were, about half the time you lost a load.

Fargo and Jennifer started into the rocks. The trail became a groove. Every vertical surface within reach was adorned with names and dates and assorted other messages. People passing through had just felt compelled to announce the fact. Some just used lead pencils, others scratched their proclamations, and a few even dug out chisels.

Jennifer scribbled notes for an hour, until they reached the top. As the wind howled and swirled, she asked about the tiny blue pyramid to the west.

"Laramie Peak," Fargo explained. "It's at least eighty miles away."

"But it looks so much closer," Jennifer protested.

"That can fool you out in this dry air. I was with some folks once over on the Mormon Trail, which runs on the north side of the river. They thought they'd just stroll over one morning and climb Courthouse Rock. I told them it was a good dozen miles, but they insisted it couldn't be more than two miles, and off they went."

"Did they climb it?"

"No. They spent most of the day pulling themselves out of the river. They wouldn't listen to me about quicksand, either."

"Well, I'll listen to you, Skye." Her tone was now more sober, recalling the graves she had seen. "This is dangerous country, isn't it?" Then she changed the subject, somewhat. "What do you make of those notes that Josiah Abernathy signed, Skye?"

"He doesn't worry me all that much, because he's not around. I gather he stays pretty much in New York, and I don't plan to go there."

"But he sent men out to kill you. And they attacked me. Doesn't that bother you?"

"They had other things to do, too, such as replacing this Arkins fellow. I don't know whether that attack on you at Kearny was something they just did, or whether it was a way to draw me in so they could get at me."

"I cannot believe your arrogance, Skye. Men. The only thing they think about is themselves. Here I'm the one who was jumped from the shadows and then assaulted, and you say it might have been just a ploy to trap you."

She caught her breath for more tirade, but Fargo interrupted. "Look, they had written orders to kill me. All I'm saying is that I don't know whether it was plain old lechery or some kind of wily scheming that inspired them to grab you." He regarded the swell of her bosom and the agreeable curve of her legs, and made sure she noticed. "Have it your way. It was pure, simple burning desire for your splendid body, Jennifer. I understand their motives perfectly."

She reddened and became interested in admiring the landscape as they dropped. The road twisted in hairpins to avoid the heads of the precipitous gullies that started up here. One gulch held a smashed wagon and four mule carcasses, still fresh enough to draw flies.

When the ground leveled, they were almost at the front door of the Scott's Bluff Station. It was a home station, where riders laid over between runs.

Even so, it wasn't all that big. Just two fair-sized dirt-roofed soddies. The front one had a makeshift porch, cobbled from the juniper that grew up on the bluffs.

In its shadows sat one of the thinnest men Fargo had ever seen, not much more than bones and skin. He had shoulder-length blond hair, and he had a jug. Since his wave didn't look like an invitation, Fargo didn't go any closer.

He knew that the Scott's Bluff Station offered no accommodations for overnight travelers, even though it had a room for Pony Express riders. The Overland stage stopped at Scott's Bluff for a one-hour dinner, then proceeded a dozen miles to Horse Creek to halt for the night.

Since Jennifer had been hinting that she could use a real bath, Fargo decided to press on to Horse Creek and get her a room. Then he'd return to Scott's Bluff and find out what he could. It meant some backtracking, but he needed to get Jennifer out of his way for a while.

In less than two hours of easy riding, they crossed Little Kiowa Creek, whose clouds of mosquitoes were just as hungry this time as they had been in previous visits, then reined up at Horse Creek Station.

"She'll need a room and some dinner," Fargo explained to the old Creole trader who ran the place, Reynal. If he had any other names, nobody knew them.

Reynal's lined face nodded. "We have room inside for the woman. Men sleep over in the barn." He pointed to what looked more like a tumbledown ruin, a slab-sided structure that lacked even a door.

"I'll take my chances with the night air. And I won't be here for dinner. I've got errands to run," Fargo said.

But he didn't turn right around. Reynal's squaw wife was nothing to look at, but their half-breed daughter combined the best features of both races. She had curves in all the right places as she sashayed around the main room, helping her mother.

Reynal caught the gleam in Fargo's eye and shot him a look that said he really ought to start thinking about something else. Besides that, the girl and her mother retired to the kitchen.

Resigned, Fargo carried Jennifer's gear to the side room where women travelers slept on floor pallets, while Jennifer stood outside the kitchen door, watching women grind corn, right on the dirt floor. The encrusted knives they used for slicing meat and bread hadn't been washed in years.

"I believe I shall get ill if I eat here," Jennifer whispered as she rejoined Fargo.

"Then don't. There's jerky and parched corn in your gear."

She made a face.

When they returned to the main room, Reynal asked if Fargo could use a drink. It was so watered that a gallon of it wouldn't have made a dwarf tipsy. Reynal had the gall to charge a whole quarter for it.

Fargo excused himself to ride the twelve miles back to Scott's Bluffs. When he arrived, the shadows were growing long and the bone-thin man still sat on the porch.

"You Arkins?" Fargo asked as he got a better look. This Arkins was mighty young; his sunburned face lacked any lines of age.

"No," came the laconic drawl from a kid who looked rather insulted. "He's in his room if you want him. He's just the agent."

"And what are you?" Fargo stepped back. He hadn't meant to affront the kid, who looked angry.

"Not some piss-ant ribbon clerk. I'm Bill Cody, and I'm the fastest damn rider on the whole Pony Express."

Fargo stuck out his hand. "Sorry for the mistake, Bill. I'm Skye Fargo."

Cody accepted his handshake. "You rode by earlier today, with a gal, didn't you?"

"That I did," Fargo agreed. "I thought you riders spent all your time in the saddle."

"Like any other job," Cody grunted, trying to sound older than his fourteen or fifteen years. "You spend time waiting, too. The westbound should be here any old time, and then I race off to Horseshoe Creek, then turn around as soon as the eastbound arrives. Then it's back to laying over here till there's more mail to move." He stooped and picked up the jug of corn liquor. After a healthy swallow, he passed it to Fargo.

"I know a lady that would like to talk to you sometime." Fargo hoisted the jug like a thirsty man, but only sipped. He wanted to be sociable, but he also wanted to keep his wits close at hand. "She's writing about the Pony Express for some New York paper, and she keeps saying she'd like to talk to some of the riders."

Cody swallowed hard. "No, I don't think I'd like that. I just want to do my job, and do it right. I don't never want to be famous or nothin' like that. Who knows what would happen if your name got in the papers?"

"Know what you mean," Fargo agreed. "I kind of got stuck with her, and part of the deal was that she wouldn't use my name, either."

Cody lightened the jug and set it on the stump beside him. "You did say you were looking for Arkins, didn't you?"

Fargo nodded.

Cody was flushed from whiskey, and he started to talk more readily than he might have otherwise. "Can't really imagine why anybody would be looking for Arkins. He's nigh worthless."

"How's that?" Fargo kept a poker face to keep from betraying his eagerness to learn more about Arkins.

"It's his job to sort the local express here, and he's slower than molasses in January. Hell, everywhere else it gets done in about three minutes, and when he goes into a room with that mochila, it sometimes takes him half an hour. Know what I think?"

"Guess I don't," Fargo allowed.

"I think he don't know how to read none too good. Why the company put a man like that in charge of sorting the local dispatches, I'll never know. Bet it takes him a good five minutes to look at an address and figure out whether it says Scott's Bluff or not. I told ol' Ficklin last time he come through on an inspection, and he said he'd try to see that Stick got transferred to some other job. But it's been a month, and Stick's still at it, pokin' along like he's got all the time in the world."

Fargo recalled the note. "Replace Arkins," it had said. Maybe Arkins didn't know the man who was supposed to replace him. If that was the case, then Fargo might be able to step in. And if it wasn't the case, Fargo had a pistol.

"Well, Bill, your wish has come true," Fargo informed Cody. "I'm supposed to replace Arkins. But I got to talk to him first."

"He's out back. Want me to take you to him?"

"No. Better if I tend to this myself." Fargo stepped through the door. The main room extended the full width of the station, about thirty feet. About ten feet deep, it served as the kitchen and dining area. A homely middle-aged woman was wrestling with pots, getting dinner ready for the expected arrival of the stage, due in shortly after sundown.

Three doors dotted the back wall of the main room. Two were open. The middle one obviously led to the woman's room, since it was neat and even had a chest of drawers. The left one had to be for laid-over Pony Express riders like Cody; it looked as though a windstorm had swept through it, with clothes and bedding lying every which way. The right door was shut; that had to be Arkins' room.

"Mr. Arkins up now?" Fargo asked the woman.

She nodded. "He just came out and got some coffee. He's going over accounts. Would you like some coffee?"

Fargo would, so he accepted the steaming enameled tin cup before rapping on the door.

"What is it? Cody, I told you not to bother me none while I was trying to catch up on the accounts."

"I'm not Cody," Fargo explained. "Need to talk to you private."

Arkins' exasperated sigh could be heard clearly through the door. A book slammed shut, papers shuffled, the tambours of a rolltop desk protested their journey before thudding closed. "All right, come on in."

Fargo stepped in. Before he noticed much else about Arkins, he noticed the snub-nosed bulldog pistol pointed at his chest. The man was sitting at a rolled-down rolltop desk, turned in his chair so that he had a view of the door and an easy shot.

"You always greet people that way?" Fargo couldn't think of anything else to say, and he knew that, much as he wanted to, reaching for his gun was not a good idea at the moment.

Arkins grunted. With his free hand, he motioned for Fargo to come on inside and to shut the door behind him. He complied and got a better look at Arkins.

He could have passed for Cody's older brother. He was just as thin, although perhaps not quite as tall—no way to tell unless he stood up. His shoulder-length hair looked darker, although that could be just an effect of being indoors, where the only light came through an oilcloth window. His hand looked too frail to hold a pistol, even this one, almost as small as a derringer.

"Man can't be any too careful these days," Arkins intoned. "There's valuable papers here, stuff strangers ought not to see. Now, who are you and what do you want?"

Fargo made himself look nervous, which wasn't hard, given the circumstances, with his back to the door and a gun pointed at him. "Jethro Hoon. I received some orders at Kearny that said I was supposed to replace you here. You're to go to Box Elder."

Arkins relaxed his hold on the pistol and lowered its muzzle, although it was still ready for immediate use. "That ain't quite the way I heard it was going to happen. Willie Lane was supposed to be the man."

Fargo shrugged. "He ran into some trouble at Kearny, I heard, and ended up on the wrong side of a blade. He's still there, and he will be forevermore."

The thin man sighed. "Shit. Willie was good at this stuff. Damn good. But you must be just as good, or they wouldn't have sent you, right?"

Fargo nodded enthusiastically, although he had no idea what it was that Willie Lane had been good at. He hadn't been real skilled at rape or shooting, that's for sure. "Right," Fargo agreed.

Arkins motioned toward a chair by the bed, seven or eight feet from his desk, and motioned for Fargo to take a seat.

Fargo took it. "They didn't tell me a whole lot about how things worked out here," he deadpanned. "Maybe you can fill me in some."

The lean face regarded Fargo with some wonderment. "You sure don't look the type. You look more like a frontiersman than a forger. If I didn't know better, I'd bet cash money that you handled a pistol a whole lot better than you handled a pen. But what the hell, you can't tell what's in a package by its wrapper, I reckon."

Fargo chuckled and provided a man-to-man smile, figuring that would improve Arkins' disposition. "Yeah, I've met a lady or two like that. They smile hungry, and bat their eyes, and breathe real deep, like they can't wait to shuck their duds. Then it turns out they're colder than a January norther."

A hint of a smile lifted Arkins' thin-lipped mouth. "Just goes to show you, I suppose." His eyes flitted at the closed desk before returning to Fargo. "What all did they tell you?"

"Not much." Fargo shifted so that he had an easier reach for his throwing knife in his boot. The tension had eased somewhat, but he was still a long ways from feeling comfortable. "They were in kind of a hurry, likely on

126

account of Willie's untimely demise. Just sent word that I was to replace you here, and to increase Consolidated Ophir with a delay and rush the results on."

"That's gonna be quite a chore." Arkins mulled for a minute. "Just how do I know you're who you say you are? Hate to be this way, but a man can't be too careful these days. That damn Ficklin pulls all kinds of tricks when he's out inspectin'."

Fargo had never met Benjamin Ficklin, but he was already starting to like the guy. He reached toward his pocket, then saw Arkins tighten his grip on the small pistol. "Easy there, Stick. I'm just reaching for a piece of paper." Fargo pulled out the note and handed it over.

Still maintaining his hold on the gun, Arkins unfolded it and examined it. His face went pale as he got to the bottom. "Jesus. That came right from the top, didn't it?"

Fargo nodded. His hope that Arkins' tongue had been loosened was rewarded. "Let me tell you. All I ever did for him was hold some of his own mail over for a week. Then they wanted me to start making up some stuff."

Fargo was puzzled, but he tried not to let that show. Arkins handed the paper back and opened the desk. Several dozen bottles of ink jammed its pigeonholes, along with an assortment of paper and a variety of writing implements—pencils, quill pens, steel-point nibs.

"Think I put together most of the gear you'll need, anyway. But I sure couldn't get the hang of it."

The outer room got noisy, and through the window came the clamor of an arriving stagecoach. Arkins pulled the desktop down and stood up. "Guess we can go over that after dinner. Got to feed these passengers, then send 'em on over to Horse Creek for the night. Mayhaps I can talk Billy Cody into helping change the horses. That little shit ought to make himself useful between runs, don't you think?"

Fargo nodded and opened the door. He got into the

main room about ten seconds before the first passengers did.

Two men led the way, and they were stomping like they were in a hurry to go hunt some supper, since they had their guns out.

"That's him," the husky black-bearded one shouted to his companion, a clean-shaven man of medium build who sported a wicked scar that started at his forehead, glowed down past his eye, across his cheek, and continued to his neck. "Get him."

Caught almost flat-footed, Fargo elected to duck first and draw later. As the woman shrieked, he dived for some cover under the oilcloth-covered table. A bullet whistled past his ear on the way down, and another plowed into a table leg. As cover went, this wasn't much, but it at least gave him time to get his gun out.

From where he sat, all he could see was boots and legs. When one buckskinned knee bent, he put a bullet into him. Scarface came tumbling down, pistol firing. The shot thudded into the packed-dirt floor, inches from Fargo's boots. The puff of dust, along with the growing cloud of powder smoke, made accuracy a matter of guesswork. Fargo's round tore out a bleeding chunk of Scarface's shoulder.

"Goddamn it, he's down here," Scarface shouted, just in case anybody hadn't figured that out yet.

"It's gotta be him," his bearded companion agreed. "It was his horse outside, and he fits perfect."

In obvious agony, Scarface gritted and got his pistol up. Fargo's bullet slammed into the man's gritted teeth, spraying fragments amid a shower of blood. The back of the man's head skipped across the dirt. Fargo couldn't see anything else worth caring about that way, so he turned in his crouch, bumping his head against the table.

Then the table flew away, tipping behind him. He had no cover, save for some powder smoke. That was enough so that Blackbeard's shot sailed wide of his head by about three inches, its hot breath passing Fargo's ear before the slug stuck in the overturned table.

The Trailsman's snap shot went right between the man's legs, and a shot came from his left, likely from Arkins and his baby gun, since it wasn't as loud as the others.

It was one gun against two, and Fargo was totally exposed. He let his pistol fall as he lunged forward like a springing panther, tackling Blackbeard at the knees. He was hoping that Arkins would be too confused to fire into the two of them as they wrestled.

This was the reverse of a normal fight, since Fargo wanted to get on bottom and have Blackbeard covering him from any shots from Arkins. He rolled as Blackbeard fell, and tried to use their momentum to get over by the wall.

Blackbeard flailed with his pistol. Its barrel chopped Fargo's hip, and it would leave a nasty bruise if he stayed alive long enough to enjoy it. Fargo used an elbow for a rabbit punch and grappled for a bear hug from behind. He succeeded enough to where he could indulge in looking at the room for a moment.

Several other stage passengers jammed the door, craning their necks to watch the battle. Over by the stove, the woman was hollering at them to scatter, but they weren't having any of that. She was pressed against the wall and started to hunker down to present less area for any stray bullets.

Still standing by his door, Arkins sent a wide bullet toward Fargo and Blackbeard.

"Goddamnit, Stick," Blackbeard roared, "don't be shootin' this way till he's in front."

Blackbeard thrashed back with his elbows, trying to break Fargo's grip. This was something of a standoff. From behind, Fargo couldn't do much to Blackbeard, and he couldn't do much to Fargo, either, except try to roll them to where Fargo would be exposed for a shot from Arkins.

The husky man was big enough to do it, too. Fargo stretched his legs out for leverage and still felt himself start to go. He tugged back, Blackbeard increased his force, then Fargo instantly snapped off his grip. Blackbeard rolled forward. With one hand, Fargo tossed a dusty clump of floor at Arkins. With the other, he planted his knife in Blackbeard's back, dead center. It went in hard, slicing the man's spine on its way, as well as an artery that sent a gusher of lifeblood toward the low ceiling.

Arkins blinked, fired, and sidestepped toward the stove to get away from the surging Trailsman. Fargo shifted stride and ducked for his pistol. The way the table had fallen, it would cover him. Colt in hand, he crawfished to the edge, rather than standing, which Arkins would be expecting.

That was just enough of an edge for Fargo to get in two hurried rounds. That woman was still over there somewhere, and if justice was to be done to these stage-station cooks, they should be poisoned with something slow and painful, not merely shot. His first round grazed Arkins' shoulder, and the second expanded his belly button.

Fargo's Colt was empty, and there wasn't time to re-load. As the gut-shot Arkins tried to settle his quivering hand, Fargo sprang forward and kicked the gun away. He shouldered Arkins back. There was a hiss and sizzle, as if someone had just thrown a steak into a hot skillet.

Arkins thrashed like a fresh-caught trout.

"I'll back up if you want to finish explaining matters to me, Stick," Fargo whispered as Arkins' skinny butt began to char. This was as good a time as any to get some more answers.

But then Stick Arkins died. That was the only reasonable explanation, anyway, for sagging back onto the cook stove's scorching surface.

11

Fargo tossed Stick Arkins' charred body to the dirt floor, got his back to a sod wall, and reloaded while waiting for the smoke to settle. He had just rammed the last bullet into its chamber when he heard a woman ask if it was safe to stand up now.

"Far as I know." He stepped over and offered the cook a hand. The heavyset woman accepted. "Excuse me," Fargo apologized. "I should have introduced myself earlier. I'm Skye Fargo."

The plump cook surveyed her stove and shambles of a dining room before returning her eyes to his. "Mary Wilford." She checked her pots, adjusted some lids and locations, then tried to right the tipped-over table.

Fargo helped her with that, then checked the door to see what had become of the other stage passengers, who weren't there anymore. "I'll be back in a minute and help you finish cleaning up this mess." He waved at the three corpses. "As soon as I see what happened to the passengers."

Out on the porch, Cody was just sitting up and dazedly rubbing a bump on the back of his head that was the size of a robin's egg and growing toward hen or maybe ostrich proportions. No one else was in sight.

"What the hell happened out here, Bill?"

The kid reached for the jug and drained at least three fingers' worth before answering. "Stage come in, so the

131

driver and I started changing the teams. Then I heard the ruckus inside. Went to shoo the passengers away from the door, and next thing I know, I'm trying to wake up and my head feels like somebody drove a bridge spike into it."

"What happened to the stage and the other passengers?"

"They took off, just as I was gettin' my eyes open, couple minutes ago."

"Weren't the passengers a bit peeved about missing dinner?"

By grasping Fargo's extended hand, Cody got to his feet before replying. "Can't say. Odd bunch. All seven of 'em looked kind of hard-case, if you catch my drift. And the driver was somebody I'd never seen before."

Fargo hollered in to advise the cook that tonight's patrons had moved on, then mulled on the stagecoach's arrival and hurried departure. Blackbeard and Scarface, the two men he'd just shot inside, had obviously been looking for him. They'd recognized his Ovaro outside and had come in with guns drawn, ready to shoot him on sight.

It made sense that they were all working for somebody. Who, then?

It had to be Josiah Abernathy. The millionaire had tentacles everywhere. He must have somehow caught wind of what Fargo was up to, and decided to put a halt to it. But why? What was Abernathy really up to?

He'd been the one to put the squeeze on Alex Majors about delayed dispatches. Stick Arkins had been the one to delay the dispatches, and Fargo felt some consolation that he had solved that problem. But Arkins seemed to have been in cahoots with Abernathy to delay those dispatches. And now there were apparent plans for forgery. Fargo wished to hell that Arkins hadn't died. If the man's live flesh had been smoking on that stove for a few more minutes, he'd have likely explained everything.

Fargo's further ruminations were disturbed by the wail of a horn in the distance.

Cody took a few deep breaths, rubbed his head one more time, and jammed his broad-brimmed hat atop it. "That's the westbound rider, Fargo. My turn to ride, on to Horseshoe Creek. If the eastbound is on time, I'll be back tomorrow."

As the westbound rider approached, Fargo and Cody rushed to saddle a bay gelding. They had it around front when the arriving rider, a towheaded kid just over five feet tall, pulled up in a cloud of dust and tossed the *mochila* to Fargo.

It had been his job, one way or another, to replace Arkins, he figured. And he was a company contractor. Fargo stepped inside, where the light was better, and opened the unsealed pouch. It held about a dozen envelopes—three for Julesburg and the rest for points east. Nothing was addressed to Scott's Bluff, so he snapped it shut and threw it over Cody's fresh horse. Moments later, he had vanished into the darkening twilight.

The new rider introduced himself as Chet Ruffin. "Mary's stew smells mighty good," he continued. He got to the door, looked inside, and turned to face the Trailsman. "Jesus, what happened in there?"

Fargo explained.

Ruffin understood why Scarface and Blackbeard were dead, but seemed suspicious about the death of the station agent. He was thinking out loud. "Don't know if I hold with that," he drawled. "Can't imagine one of our agents being a turncoat." He paused. " 'Course, if Bill Cody thinks you were in the right here, mister, then I reckon that's good enough for me. He seen it all, and I didn't."

Fargo didn't bother to mention how little Cody had actually seen. They dragged the bodies out, with plans to bury them in the morning. The moon was full, providing enough light for that work, but digging graves by moonlight under the looming bluffs sounded like a dismal chore. Then they settled down to an ample dinner, better than most at stagecoach eating stops. The meat was fresh, from an antelope Cody had shot yesterday. Mary Wilford baked light, flaky biscuits that weren't raw in the middle. Her coffee was real coffee, not some mixture of old grounds and chickory bark. She even provided a few fresh greens from her garden, and they weren't cooked beyond recognition into the usual mush.

As far as everybody present was concerned, Fargo was now the acting agent for Scott's Bluff Station. So, after the dinner chatter while Mary cleared the table and washed dishes, he headed back to Arkins' room. Maybe something in the man's desk would explain just what had been going on here.

He pushed the door open, saw the lamp atop the desk, and pulled out a match. He pulled the glass chimney off, adjusted the wick, and got it going. He replaced the chimney and plopped into the chair. He reached to open the rolltop when a bullet sliced through the oilcloth window and shattered the lamp.

Fargo instinctively dropped to the floor, amid a spreading pool of burning coal oil. The eager flames lapped at his buckskin fringes. He wasn't too worried that a sod building would go up in flames, but it was still a good idea to keep fire in its place, and this wasn't its place.

His buckskins protected him from anything worse than momentary discomfort as he rolled around the floor, smothering the flames. Still the room was bright, and when he looked up, the top of the oaken desk was starting to crackle. The black smoke of coal oil was being replaced by the cleaner smoke from burning wood.

The desk likely held any hope he had of solving all this. He turned to see Ruffin at the door, crouched but poised to heave the slop bucket at the flaming desk.

"No," Fargo hollered. "Don't!" Pouring water where there was burning oil would generally just spread the fire, unless you were real lucky. And besides, water would ruin the papers inside, just as surely as a fire would if it got there. But if Fargo tried to smother the fire, he'd collect a painful assortment of burns, if he didn't get shot just for sticking his head up.

He crawfished over to Arkins' bed and tugged at a buffalo robe. It had to weigh at least fifty pounds, and the leverage was working against him, since he was on the floor. Fargo sat up against the bed and snapped the robe over his head. His massive shoulders propelled the heavy hide across the small room, and it settled atop the desk, covering all but one edge.

Ruffin caught on and leapt over, hat extended. He slammed it down atop the flames, amid another whistle through the oilcloth. He sagged against the wall and extended an arm to his hat on the desktop, trying to stay upright. Then he collapsed, a hole between his sightless eyes.

There wasn't a thing Fargo could do for him. Fargo realized that if he stood up, the light from the lamp in the main room would silhouette him against the oilcloth. Nothing was stirring in the main room, but that just meant that the cook was staying low. Fargo crawled to the door between Arkins' room and the main room.

She wasn't by the stove. He eased over, out of the line of sight of that back window, and began to rise.

So did Mary Wilford, from behind the table, whose oilcloth covering hung nearly to the floor. She held a quart-sized tin kettle of scalding hot water, and she flung it straight toward Fargo.

He ducked and sidestepped to miss most of it. The kettle clanked against the wall as a few hot drops stung his face. His blinking eyes stayed open as he adjusted his crouch. "Mary, we're on the same side here."

"Oh no we aren't." She rose from behind the table. Instead of a kettle, this time she was holding a light Colt navy pistol, the same one that Scarface had been carrying. She was not upset. Her hands weren't even trembling as she pointed its muzzle at his chest, only a dozen feet away.

"You killed my man, Skye Fargo."

"Stick Arkins was your man?" She'd make three of him, easy. They must have been like Jack Spratt, who ate no fat, and his wife who ate no lean. But there were two rooms here, one for her and one for him. That didn't stand to reason.

She nodded and seemed to be able to read the question in Fargo's mind. "We didn't let on that we was married. Less likely that way that people'd think we worked together."

"Worked together at what? Tending a station. Lots of married folks do that. She cooks and he handles the rest."

The woman laughed without humor. "More to it than that, Fargo. More than you'll ever know. You ride in here, you killed my man. But you're not going to kill our dreams. Stick may not be here, but I'll continue his work."

"Just who are you working for anyway? If it's Russell, Majors and Waddell, I've got some news for you that might change your mind."

She thumbed the hammer back with an ominous click. "Oh, I know all about you. You're just some company snoop like that wretched Mr. Ficklin, who thinks he's so important because he works for such a big company. Russell, Majors and Waddell look like big frogs in a big pond. But it's Mr. Josiah Abernathy who's going to own the pond, and I'm on his side. He rewards people handsomely, Fargo. I can bury you with the others, run the station here, and do whatever Mr. Abernathy needs to have done."

The woman smiled in a mean, satisfied way that made Fargo feel even more disgusted. Here he was, crouched against a wall, pinned down by a cocked revolver held by a fat cook who was starting to cackle as she gloated about getting the drop on him. If he even thought about reaching for his own gun, he was as good as dead.

But she couldn't be all that experienced at shooting people in cold blood, or she wouldn't have been taking so much time, as if she were talking herself into the necessity of shooting him.

"Ruffin," Fargo shouted, snapping his head toward the door.

She moved her eyes that way, giving Fargo enough time to come up shooting. Maybe it was just tension or maybe there was something inside him that kept him from shooting to kill when he was firing at a woman. His shot just grazed her shoulder, moments after her own shot thudded into the wall behind where Fargo had just been.

The woman dropped instantly, tilting the table so she had some cover to continue firing toward him. The safest place was directly on the other side of the table, where her waving gun wouldn't reach. Fargo plunged that way.

His legs stuck out behind him, enough so that her next shot tore off a piece of his boot heel. He pulled his legs up behind him and nudged at the six-foot-long table, to get some idea of her exact position. Then he raised his hand with his Colt pointed down. It was either that or try sending a bullet through two inches of close-grained maple.

He pulled the trigger. His round hit her somewhere, because he heard it splat into flesh, followed by a screech. He thumb-cocked for another round and found it impossible to hold on to the gun, because a whirring butcher knife had just sliced his wrist, and his blood was flying out in a pulsing spray that nearly blinded him as he jerked his arm back.

He jammed the wrist against his midsection, hoping the pressure would stop the bleeding. The flow slowed a bit, but the stain continued to grow on his buckskin shirt. He knew he was about ten minutes from bleeding to death unless he somehow bandaged the gaping wound to stanch this lethal leakage of his lifeblood.

Even worse, he'd given her an idea. Her revolver peeked over the tabletop and sent a shot down, just missing his hip. Instinctively he lifted his right hand to swipe at her pistol when it peeked over again, and he bled like a crimson waterfall. He stuck the wrist under his left arm-pit and jammed his arm tight. Now he couldn't move either arm without hastening his own death. Already he felt light-headed, and he was sitting in a pool of his own sticky blood that hadn't finished seeping into the dirt floor.

Fargo shifted so he could at least hold his belt knife in his hand. He might be able to do what she did to stop those over-the-edge shots. If he could move his hands fast enough and do that without letting himself bleed some more . . . This was not a good day to die, nor a good way to die, but he was running out of choices.

His shoulder sagged against the table. It skidded an inch or two. Fat as Mary was, he did outweigh her enough to force the table to move. But what the hell good would that do?

Force her back, to where she'd have to jump out into the open. Of course, she had a gun, and he didn't. But he did have the throwing knife. He'd have but an instant; he'd have to stick her before she could fire at him. And he'd have to throw it left-handed. No, he could use his right for that long, one swift cast. Once he didn't have to worry about somebody trying to kill him, he'd be able to bandage the wound, which was starting to hurt like somebody'd poured salt into it.

Fargo kept the pressure on the tilted tabletop. If she thought he was trying to roll it over on her, then maybe she wouldn't try shooting at him for the few seconds it took to pull the throwing knife out of his boot.

He had to release his right wrist from his left armpit to place the knife in his right hand, which was working rather grudgingly. He hoped no vital muscles or nerves had been sliced, because that hand had to work right if he was ever going to walk out of here, and he sure as hell didn't want to be carried out.

The bleeding wasn't very bad now, just a seep. The shallow three-inch gash was starting to close. Fargo shouldered the table her way some more, every sense alert for the moment that she would pop up and start shooting.

She didn't. Progress was slow and ponderous, then came to a dead halt. Had one of the legs jammed against something? No, the legs were on his side. Maybe she'd turned, so her back was to the tabletop, and she had her feet planted against the wall, with her knees locked. That would prevent more motion, although the top edge should still rock a bit. It did.

Fargo felt better, until he checked his bearings and realized they were still too far from the wall for her to have her feet against it. So how was she stopping it?

The cast-iron stove. It stuck out about four feet from the wall, which seemed about the right distance here. Wouldn't her feet be getting hot if they were pressed against the stove's feet, though?

No, likely not. She wore stout shoes, and the legs at the bottom of a stove didn't generally get all that hot anyway. She'd be able to hold on for quite a while. Maybe long enough for him to bleed to death.

But nobody wants to get jammed against a hot stove. Fargo shouldered even harder with what strength he had left. He dug his boots into the floor and strained. Nothing happened. He was right behind her. Maybe if he shifted, then he could rotate the table and get her out in the open, where he had his one chance.

He shook the sweat out of his eyes and mulled on that. Then he realized that the tabletop wasn't one solid piece of maple. It was made of planks, each about a foot wide. If he poked her through a crack, then she'd have to move. And when she moved, he could roll the table over on top of her and lay atop the heavy boards until she quit wriggling and breathing. And if she somehow escaped . . . Well, he'd need the throwing knife then.

Gingerly Fargo pushed the knife through the lower of the two cracks. When he estimated that its tip had reached the other side, he thrust it forward savagely. Its honed point met little resistance in the instant that it took to slice through a calico shift, a cotton chemise, the woman's skin, some lard, and a whole bunch of tender nerves.

She screamed and tried to bolt forward, away from the table. Fargo's knife tore down the small of her back and gouged her rump as she struggled forward and the table began to roll atop her. Thrashing furiously, she freed herself from the knife and escaped the turning table by pulling herself up.

The only thing she had to grab to pull herself up was the stovetop. Fargo could hear her hands sear against the hot metal even as he rolled with the table. He twisted his head and saw her falling atop him, blood trickling from her rear and her blistered hands pawing at the air. Even in her desperate agony, she was bent on killing him. Her feet alit next to his head and she got in a kick that would have shamed an angry mule.

Mindful to keep his wrist clamped beneath his armpit, Fargo rolled away while the woman screamed curses and looked desperately for a weapon. He gritted his teeth and hoped this wouldn't kill him. In a spray of his own blood from his gashed wrist, Fargo cast the slender throwing knife at the woman's wattled throat.

For a moment, she stood there gape-mouthed, stopped in the middle of screeching something terrible about Fargo's mother. Then a rosy froth bubbled at her lips and she collapsed. Even in that, she was steadfast in her lust to kill the man who had ruined her dreams. She fell so that most of her considerable weight crashed into his ribs.

Fargo caught his breath and sidled out from under her. There were times to be gentlemanly, perhaps, but this wasn't one of them. With his left hand, he pulled his knife out of her throat and set to work on her petticoat, hacking out bandages.

There were noises outside. Shit. With all this surprise hostility from somebody he thought was on the same side, he'd totally forgotten that there were people outside who'd been shooting in. Chet Ruffin, Pony Express rider, deserved better than that.

Now that he wasn't in imminent danger of bleeding to death, Fargo took stock. He found his own heavy Colt, with just two shots left in it. Mary's was empty. He was out of powder and balls; the gear was with the Ovaro, and the Ovaro was outside. So was his Sharps.

Maybe he could sneak out there in the night and get them. But once he got to his horse, why the hell would he want to stay in here? And besides, the moon was shining, and there were men out there with guns who shot at the shadows on the oilcloth. He realized that the only reason they hadn't fired during his struggle with the cook was that they hadn't wanted to hit her, one of their allies. Besides, they'd been too low to cast silhouettes through most of it, anyway.

But this was a stage station, wasn't it? They'd have to keep a few guns around somewhere. He didn't remember any. He scanned the walls, just to be sure. All that was up there was a lamp on a shelf, which illuminated Mary's bloody corpse.

Hunkering low and moving slow, Fargo went back to

Stick's room, where a heavy wooden steamer trunk sat by the bed. If he could get his hands on some weapons, then he could stand off the besiegers until morning. If not, they could charge anytime, and he'd be a sitting duck.

The trunk was locked, so it took him several minutes to worry it open with his knife. Every sweating second, he thought he heard whispers outside. The latch opened. Fargo swung the top up and had to feel for the contents, since the shadows were so deep that he couldn't see.

Good. The place was equipped to stand off a raid by Indians or outlaws. The trunk held half a dozen .50-caliber Maynard carbines. It wasn't Fargo's favorite gun, but he was familiar with it, since the Maynard was standard issue for the U.S. cavalry on the plains. He felt around and found several boxes of paper cartridges and heavy bags of bullets.

Nobody with any sense stored percussion caps in the same place as the powder-laden cartridges. Fargo found a tin full of caps in a desk drawer. Working mostly by feel, he loaded four of the carbines, all he could carry, and eased back to the main room, his pockets full of ammunition.

That wasn't a lot of exertion, but he'd lost a quart of blood. He felt light-headed and drowsy, in a perfect mood for falling asleep. There was still coffee on the stove, so he crawled over there on all fours and got himself a cup, without ever sticking his head up. As long as the lamp was going, he didn't dare stand.

He considered dowsing the lamp. But he'd have to stand up to do that. And any apparent change in here might bring the outside men, whoever they were, charging in at him. The rifles would help, but a fight in the room would be at close quarters, where pistols were more effective. They'd have pistols, and he wouldn't. Best to stall for time.

After all, Scott's Bluffs sat right on the major east-west route of North America. Scott's Bluff Station was visited daily by a stage going in each direction. Pony Express riders stopped here. Somebody would be along sometime tomorrow. Those men couldn't hold this station under siege forever. He could outwait them.

Fargo arranged a fortress for himself in a corner. He had the tilted table before him, and it was thick enough to stop anything smaller than a Sharps bullet; he would be protected from pistol shots. Behind him was one window, so he could shoot out or escape if necessary and possible. He had the water bucket with its dipper, so he wouldn't go thirsty for a spell. He had four carbines, all loaded, and enough ammunition for a small war.

Trusting his hair-trigger nerves to rouse him, Fargo nodded off for several hours. When he came 'round, it was because there was some shouting outside. Groggily, he realized that somebody was bellowing his name from outside the oilcloth window, which was pale gray with the first glimmers of dawn.

"Hey, Fargo, ain't you gonna look outside?"

The voice was coming from the porch. He remained silent.

"Come on, Trailsman. We want you to see this."

Fargo kept his mouth shut as he heard some thrashing, then some clothes ripping, and a woman's shriek. "No, Skye, no. Stay in—"

It was Jennifer's voice until some big hand muffled it.

"Come on, Fargo, take a look. The newspaper lady's got a nice pretty pair of titties, and she told us you'd never seen them."

The steps moved away from the porch with what had to be Jennifer's feet dragging. A couple of bullets slammed into the sod wall and one pierced the oilcloth.

Fargo heard some crackling and smelled the pungent scent of burning piñon. From out there somewhere, a voice announced, "If the son of a bitch won't come out no other way, we'll smoke him out. Make sure every damn door and window's covered. We ain't got much time."

12

Tendrils of smoke swirled through the bullet holes in the oilcloth that formed the front window just above Fargo. Just in case he felt like moving, bullets were flying in through every window in the front room. Sporadic shrieks from Jennifer punctuated the steady rumble of gunfire pouring into Scott's Bluff Station.

Fargo slumped back against the wall. In this front corner he was as safe as he'd be anywhere, even if he couldn't do anything. He rolled his eyes upward as he tried to relax and think things through. There had to be a way.

The roof was so low that Fargo could touch it easily when standing flat-footed. The ceiling was unbleached muslin, to catch most of the dust, mud, and mice that might fall out of the pole-and-dirt roof right above it.

Fargo thought of what lay above him. He closed his eyes to recall the appearance of the front, above the porch, which was now starting to burn intensely. The front had extended a good two or three feet above the top of the porch. So there had to be some wall that ran above the roof. Between it and the smoke, he'd have some cover up on the roof. He'd be able to shoot back, instead of staying pinned in a corner.

He stood and sliced the muslin with his knife, then knocked down clumps of packed dirt. A brightening sky, tinged with black smoke, greeted him through the growing gap. The two poles that showed were four or five inches in diameter, somewhat more than a foot apart, and laced with twigs. He pulled down the twigs.

Normally, he might have been able to grab the poles and pull himself up. But his right wrist was still weak, and such exertion would tear the wound open. He shifted the table until a protruding leg could provide footing. He shoved a carbine up, gathered his ammunition, and eased up slowly.

While bullets still pounded into the soddy below him, Fargo got his bearings. He wasn't in any hurry to start shooting and give away his new position.

The station faced north, toward the river. Fargo hunkered against the two-foot-high wall and found a notch that would let him see out through clear spots in the smoke. Two men stood below. Several others crouched as they fired into the building. Between the two standing men was Jennifer, with her hands tied behind her back and no clothes except for her drawers, stockings, and shoes. Every so often, she would holler at Fargo to stay inside.

To the east, the giant bulwark of Scott's Bluff shielded the rising sun. Fargo couldn't be sure, given how much powder and wood smoke there was nearby, but it looked as though some dust was stirring in the gap that wagons took. But even if that was so, it didn't mean much, considering how strong and wayward the wind was up there.

Westward, paralleling the river toward Horse Creek, ran the road that he had been over twice yesterday.

Fargo turned around. About thirty yards to the south lay the stable, another sod structure. There was no hope of reaching it, because there was a rifleman on each side. The only comfort was that his Ovaro had been put in the corral with the other stock, likely because he was a valuable horse that somebody planned to take when the dust settled here. Far beyond the corral, the barren Wild-cat Hills sprawled to the south.

Every direction Fargo cared to look, there were riflemen. All told, there were a dozen, perhaps more. He had attracted the attention of an overnight army whose paymaster and strategic general had to be Josiah Abernathy. It was amazing what you could accomplish from a mansion two thousand miles away when you were the richest man in America.

Now, to even the odds before they figured out where he was. The south side looked best. Only two men were back there, one on each side of the stable, and their leaders were up front on the north side. His back to the wall, Fargo got comfortable and shouldered the carbine. He took a deep calming breath and squeezed the trigger at the man on the left side.

Fargo hadn't had a chance to test the sights, so the shot sailed high and to the right, just grazing the man's shoulder. He dropped prone, behind a rock. Fargo jammed in another round and swung the muzzle left. He adjusted for the misaligned sights by aiming at the crouching man's left hip. Moments later, the man rolled back with the force of a half-inch ball of lead that tore open his chest.

Fargo returned his attention to the wounded man. He wanted to finish him off before he could holler for help or otherwise point out that the Trailsman was now on the roof.

The man had crawled back along the stable wall, leaving a dotted trail of blood, and he was just now turning the corner. All that stuck out was his boots, not much to shoot at. The boot toes dug in, as if the man was pulling himself to his feet a little bit too early. Through his sights, Fargo hoped for something important to appear at the far corner.

What appeared a moment later was the bearded rifle-man, with a Dakota war lance stuck in his brisket, its bloody tip protruding from his back. He had his hands full as he tried to pull it out with no success. He hollered about "Injuns," but the shout was hoarse and did not attract attention from the others.

Fargo first thought his best course was to drop down the back and leg it south to the stable. Then again, there was at least one Sioux warrior back there, and Fargo had no idea what that meant. It could be just one horse thief who'd been surprised in the act, or it could be a whole raiding party hidden out there.

Besides, there were shooters at the sides. The three on the east were all prone amid clumps of sagebrush. They weren't easy targets. The only way to spot them was by their puffs of powder smoke.

But it wasn't just blue-gray smoke in the air over there. Behind them rose a considerable cloud of dust, coming from the rocks at the bottom of the pass that crossed Scott's Bluff. Fargo couldn't hear much over the gunfire, but it sure sounded like bawling steers.

Moments later, the leaders of the herd emerged. Fargo recognized the oxen in their leather shoes. As more of the thirst-crazed herd thundered out, the emigrant train's youthful wrangler pushed his horse hard, trying to get in front and turn the herd before they stumbled into the badlands between them and the river they craved.

The three prone men shooting his way hadn't noticed the cattle, likely because their ears were ringing from all their firing. Fargo gave them something else to think about as he sent bullets down their way.

His first round must have caught a shoulder or arm, because the man's rifle dropped. Fargo then creased his neighbor's rump, five yards away. The man howled in agony and looked up, confused. Bullets weren't supposed to be coming from above. Fargo was about ready to blow the man's head off, but held fire. He didn't want to kill any of the emigrants' oxen. An instant later, all three men were being pounded by hooves.

Fargo looked left and saw that the wrangler had succeeded in turning the herd away from the river badlands, back toward the road. Now about two hundred eager cattle were churning the flats.

The two men in front of the station, the apparent leaders, had seen enough. Dragging Jennifer, their hostage and perhaps shield, they were mounting and riding west. The three on the ground, who had been shooting at Fargo, were up and running toward their horses.

One tumbled down, caught in midstride by an arrow. Then a Sioux warrior, horse right behind him, jumped out of the sagebrush. Several other mounted braves seemed to materialize out of the dust and smoke.

Things seemed quieter than they should over on the west side. Fargo edged over and understood why. The three men there all lay prone with arrows sticking out of their backs. More striking were the bloody rings of mush where their scalps had been.

Fargo looked east, hoping there was some way to signal the wrangler kid that he'd best pull back before he ran into the Sioux band. Shit. It wasn't just the kid. Half the people on the train, curious about the ruckus, were now emerging from the foot of the pass.

Toward the river, Fargo spotted one last brave on horseback and recognized the man's single eagle feather and huge hatchet nose. Fargo hollered a greeting.

Red Cloud gestured with his war lance, indicating that he already knew who was on the roof and inviting Fargo to step down for a parley.

The stampeding oxen avoided the smoke of the burning porch, so there was a halfway safe place to converse in sign language. Fargo didn't think the Indians had anything against him, but he was worried about the emigrants.

"They travel with my protection, Trailsman," Red Cloud explained. "Like you, they have good hearts. When we had no food and our children were crying, you and they shared with us."

Relieved, Fargo asked about the raid.

"The man who sells bad whiskey at Horse Creek came to us in the night. We were camped across the river. He said evil men had stolen a woman from him, right out of his lodge, and that my brother the Trailsman might need help at the bluffs."

That had to be Reynal. Some of this small army must have pushed their way inside and taken Jennifer, to use her to get at Fargo. Reynal had seen that, and he must have learned of the other trouble from Bill Cody, the Pony Express rider.

Fargo and Red Cloud simultaneously looked over to see Max Schottbein, the leader of the emigrant train. He walked slowly toward them, looking apprehensive but trying to do his duty, which included figuring out what the hell was going on.

"I'm sorry, Mr. Fargo," he apologized.

"Sorry for what? That was a great idea, stampeding your oxen down here when I was surrounded."

Schottbein smiled ruefully. "It wasn't planned." He licked his lips and explained more. "Since we had a bright moon, we labored into the night to get through the pass. We found a small open area just on this side and halted about midnight. We unyoked the oxen. They were exhausted from their labors and rested peacefully. But when light came, well, there was no holding them."

"They were sure thirsty," Fargo agreed and looked downriver, where the bank was easier. The cattle were contentedly lapping up water. "In about an hour, you'll be able to drive them back and get your wagons down."

Two sets of continuing agonized screams came from the cottonwoods near the cattle. Red Cloud just smiled and shrugged, as if to say, "How am I to stop my young warriors from slowly torturing the two evil men they just captured?"

Fargo's skin crawled just thinking about it, and Schottbein looked even more edgy. Red Cloud placidly changed the subject and asked about the two men who had ridden off with Jennifer. Did Fargo want some help going after them?

"No," Fargo said. "They are mine. But I will give you their horses as a mark of my respect for a great warrior who does not forget his friends."

Now it was almost quiet, except for the diminishing wails from the grove where Red Cloud was headed. The porch was just smoldering. Fargo collected his gear and made sure everything was working, then headed west on the Ovaro, to get Jennifer away from her captors.

After two miles of familiar road, his heart sank. He was too late. Jennifer's screams from some cottonwoods near the river were even worse than what came from the two men in Sioux hands. Colt in hand, Fargo padded quietly, flitting from cover to cover, toward the source of the sounds.

In a small clearing, Jennifer sobbed furiously. A linen duster about a foot too long covered her. The duster's owner, a lean sandy-haired man even taller than the Trailsman, had an arm across her shoulder. He was trying to comfort her. "Please, miss, you'll just have to understand the ways of the West." He said more, but Fargo couldn't hear it, on account of gunshots and hideous screeching from some thick brush even closer to the river, perhaps a hundred yards away.

Fargo straightened and stepped out. "Skye," Jennifer shouted enthusiastically. "You're all right." She broke loose and ran toward him, nearly toppling him with her tackling embrace.

She shuddered against him. The tall man stepped over. "You're Fargo, I gather."

He nodded.

"Pleased to make your acquaintance. I've heard many good things about you. I'm Benjamin Ficklin."

Fargo acknowledged the greeting, since he couldn't shake hands conveniently. Jennifer's bear hug pinned his arms to his side. "I've heard plenty of good about you, too, Ficklin. What happened here?"

"I was up at Slade's station, Horseshoe Creek past Fort Laramie. Cody told us there was trouble back here, so we rode east. We got here just as two miscreants were pounding west, this lady with them. We got her away from them."

"We? Who's with you? Cody?"

"Black Jack Slade. Our rider at Horseshoe was sick with an awful fever, and the eastbound express hadn't arrived anyway, so Cody rode on west. That kid. He can ride two hundred miles easier than most men can cross a street."

"What's going on over there? Is that where Slade is?" Fargo didn't need to point to where the occasional shots and continued screaming were coming from.

"No, don't look," Jennifer whispered. "It's horrible. Even those men don't deserve that."

Fargo ignored her plea and walked with Ficklin. Jennifer, unwilling to stay by herself, came along, looking glum.

The two screaming men were tied to tree trunks, about ten feet apart. Both had gaping wounds—hands, wrists, feet, knees, thighs, shoulders. About twenty steps away, Black Jack Slade, a huge man with a chest-length black beard, was calmly reloading his revolver. He looked up.

As if he were a city swell, he elegantly doffed his wide-brimmed black hat. "Good morning again, ma'am. And top of the day to you, Mr. Ficklin." He paused and eyed Fargo. "And of course, it's always a pleasure to see the Trailsman."

It was a good thing he didn't offer to shake, because Fargo wouldn't have felt comfortable shaking hands. Black Jack Slade was either courtly, or the meanest son of a bitch in the West. There wasn't any in between with him.

Slade turned back to his work. His wide-eyed victims gasped as he spoke. "Nobody but nobody walks into one of my stations and takes a woman. Do you men understand that?" He didn't wait for an answer. "And nobody besieges one of my stations, either. Have you gentlemen figured that out yet?"

Slade fired. The right man's left wrist shattered and he screamed. Slade fired again. The left man's right leg exploded, with jagged bone fragments where there had been a shin.

Fargo had seen enough. His own Colt jumped up. With two swift shots, he put the men out of their misery. Jennifer looked at him with mixed admiration and horror, while Slade's countenance held pure anger.

"Why'd you do that, Fargo?"

He didn't answer, because there weren't any words that could make Black Jack Slade understand that even in a hard land, there were limits, limits that men had to impose upon themselves.

Hand on his own revolver, Ficklin spoke up. "Jack, you made your point. And besides, you're not the division superintendent anymore. Those aren't your stations." Slade looked even more surly as Ficklin continued. "That damn mean streak of yours is going to get you killed someday, Jack, unless you can rein it in. Now, come on. You've done your job here."

Slade sighed and grudgingly holstered his Remington. Out at the road, he said he'd head back to his own station at Horseshoe Creek, thirty miles to the west.

Ficklin said he'd like to ride back to Scott's Bluff Station with Fargo and Jennifer.

With the two outlaws' horses in tow as a gift for Red Cloud, they took it easy on the way back, just ambling along. Fargo explained what he'd learned about Stick Arkins, as well as the nature of the assignment that Alex Majors had given him in distant St. Joe.

"So it was Arkins that was causing the trouble. Well, good riddance to him. We'll get another man in there and hope he's married to a good cook, and hope too that he's honest."

They rounded a bend and saw the emigrants driving their oxen back up to their wagons on the pass. Ficklin was thinking out loud. "Say, Fargo, could you help us out for a few days here?"

"What did you have in mind?"

"Could you tend the station till I can get some new help?"

Fargo hadn't ever cared much for Scott's Bluff, and he liked the place even less now. But he was tired, his slashed wrist still throbbed, and tending this station looked like an agreeable way to loaf and stay on Majors' payroll at premium wages. "Sure," he agreed as they dismounted. Ficklin went inside to check out the damage.

Jennifer stepped over. "May I stay with you, Skye?"

Fargo shrugged. She took that to mean she should try harder. "I'll even cook. I'm not very good at it, but I couldn't be worse than the others."

For the first time in what seemed like years, Fargo laughed. "No, I suppose you couldn't. Sure. There are even separate rooms in there."

Jennifer blushed and started to stammer. Before she could say anything, Ficklin stepped out and thanked Fargo for helping the Pony Express stay in business. While they were talking, Jennifer stepped inside.

When Fargo finally got in after her, she was standing

next to the cook's bed, jaybird-naked. Her breasts were every bit as succulent as Fargo had presumed, and her nipples rose like ripe cherries. She didn't need a corset for an hourglass shape. Her smooth, flat stomach gently swelled into muscular hips that still looked soft. Her thighs rippled with the same anticipation that was written all over her face.

"Please bar the door, Skye. I don't think we want to be disturbed."

Fargo agreed with that much and took care of that chore. When he turned, she was on her back, atop the bed. Her head was cocked on a pillow, she had her knees up with her legs spread, as though Fargo needed to be pointed toward the glistening pink target that invited between her thighs.

"Skye, hurry." Her voice was a hoarse whisper.

He started shedding clothes. "What made you change your mind, Jennifer?"

"Get on top of me and I'll tell you."

She was still being a tease, but Fargo didn't mind so much now. From the foot of the bed, he rolled forward and spread toward her, landing almost in the right position. She shifted her hips just enough to accommodate his probing organ, and they began to pound together. It felt as savage as it felt smooth, and it felt plenty of both.

The world beyond this little room vanished from Fargo's consciousness. He forgot his wounded wrist. His good hand ranged over every part of that delicious body that he could reach, while she returned the favor and giggled when she wasn't gasping.

They exploded together in a fit of shuddering ecstasy. They were cuddling and comfortable when Jennifer finally explained why she had changed her mind. "I was sure I was going to be ravished after those men stole me from Horse Creek Station, especially after they ripped off my clothing."

"It was a reasonable thing to expect under the circumstances," Fargo agreed.

"I wondered if I could take it. Then I realized I could. I'd been through that before. And if I could do that with men I hated and despised, then why couldn't I enjoy it with a man I admired?"

There wasn't a reason on earth to argue with her logic, so Fargo just shifted so that she'd have an easier time grasping his tool and stroking it back into vigor. "Glad you saw it that way."

Jennifer saw it that way for about an hour more of heaving passion. But by then, there were cattle lowing outside, which meant the emigrants had finally come down. Stages were due soon, as well as a Pony Express courier. They had work to do, starting with cleaning this place out.

Fortunately, they got some help from Schottbein's grateful wagon train. It wasn't until well after sundown and feeding eight stage passengers, though, that they had any time to themselves.

"Skye, I've been thinking."

In Fargo's memory, that had never led to a woman saying anything he cared to hear. But he nodded.

"All this was Abernathy's doing, wasn't it? He created a week-long delay here for his own messages, so that he'd have leverage to use on Alex Majors, to hurt the company's financial standing, so that Abernathy could perhaps take over the Pony Express. That's the only reasonable explanation, Skye. But I can't imagine why he'd want to take over the Pony Express. It's losing money. Majors himself told me in confidence that they get ten dollars for every dispatch, but it costs thirty-eight dollars to carry one across the continent."

Fargo started to respond. "Maybe Abernathy wants to take over the Pony Express so he can be sure of getting first peek at everything that's sent."

Jennifer nodded excitedly. "That would explain it. Then Abernathy hires a gang of bandits to stop you from discovering his scheme here." Jennifer caught her breath. "The outlaws he hired this time are dead. But he can just hire more people to further his schemes, can't he?"

Fargo glumly agreed. "That's true, Jennifer. But I still haven't figured out everything that he was up to, and I don't know of any way to get to him, short of riding onto Wall Street and trying to shoot him down through his bodyguards."

Jennifer frowned. "But there has to be some way to make him pay."

Fargo mulled for a moment. "You're writing for the New York *Herald*, aren't you? Wouldn't Abernathy be ruined by a published exposé of what he's doing out here, hiring gangs of murderers and kidnappers?"

Jennifer brightened, but the more she thought, the lower her face fell. "It would be very difficult to prove a connection to Abernathy that would stand up in a courtroom, and you could be sure he would have a gang of expensive lawyers attacking any newspaper that printed such a story. And further, the *Herald* is owned and run by Bennett. Mr. Bennett may say he speaks for the common man, but I have the distinct impression that he would not go out of his way to offend a powerful millionaire. Even worse, he might just blackmail Abernathy— take money for not printing a story."

Fargo looked for the jug and found it on a shelf. He took a healthy swig. Damn. The strange New York world of publishing and high finance sounded just as vicious as anything in the West. Men wanted the same things, money and power, wherever they were; they just fought differently in cities, with weapons that Fargo wasn't familiar with.

"Maybe we could get him some other way," Fargo suggested. "Think about that note." He found it in his pocket and examined it again. "Replace Arkins, send to Box Elder. Decrease Consolidated Ophir with delay, results to me post-haste."

She looked at it while he thought out loud. "I've replaced Arkins. As for the rest, they must be expecting some kind of message about the production of the Consolidated Ophir operations in Virginia City, over on the edge of the Sierras."

Jennifer caught on and amplified Fargo's thoughts. "That's it. Abernathy wants that production report first, so he'll know how to play the stock exchange. The man here was supposed to find the Consolidated Ophir message, forge one that would decrease its stock price, and send the forged message on after a week's delay. Meanwhile, the real numbers would go to Abernathy right away."

That was why Arkins had marveled that the Trailsman didn't look like what he was expecting—a skilled forger. Fargo's penmanship wasn't anything to brag on, but Jennifer said she was willing to try.

About an hour later, Bill Cody rode in, nearly asleep in his saddle. He almost collapsed; he'd been riding constantly since Fargo had last seen him—the kid had gone at least two hundred miles. They had a fresh horse, but no rider.

"Oh, hell, I'll go on to Mud Springs," Cody muttered through his exhaustion. "Let me rest a bit while you check the *mochila*." He was so tired that he didn't recognize Fargo or Jennifer; in his condition, one station crew was pretty much the same as another.

Fargo sorted through the packet and found several likely prospects among the envelopes. Jennifer started breaking laws when she began to steam open the first envelope.

Cody rose from his chair, protesting even as his legs

threatened to collapse beneath him. "Ma'am, you can't open mail addressed to others."

Fargo got an arm around the rider's shoulders. "Just you calm down, Bill. This is all for a good cause. Here, have a drink." His other hand presented Cody with the jug, the kid's weakness. He gulped it like a drowning man gulps air. In his current exhausted state, the whiskey made him barely able to stagger to the table.

He tried to look up while Jennifer steamed open the second letter. Moments later, he was facedown and snoring gently.

"Here it is, Skye. Consolidated Ophir production reports. From the look of it, the mines are doing quite well. We're supposed to forge some lower figures?"

Fargo nodded, but then had second thoughts. "Even if those are the orders, I can't see what need there is to forge what's supposed to go out. We can just delay it a week and send something different out to Abernathy right away."

"I see." Jennifer was on her way to the rolltop desk. She began examining paper and writing implements. "I should think we would want to give Abernathy information that indicated Consolidated Ophir stock was due to drop. That way, he would sell short, and he'll get caught."

She knew Wall Street, and Fargo knew mining. "Cut the tonnage figures in half. Mention that assays show the new veins running only forty ounces to the ton. Point out that they're going to need a lot of capital, real soon, to install pumps, because they're running into water as they go deeper. And for good measure, hint at some labor unrest, that some dangerous agitators among the miners are complaining that men ought not to break their backs and risk their lives for twelve hours a day, six days a week, for fifteen dollars a week."

While Fargo offered Cody more whiskey every time the youth stirred, Jennifer went to work with pen and paper. She got it right on her third try. They sealed it and addressed another dispatch to Abernathy, indicating that Skye Fargo would no longer trouble them. They repaired the damaged envelopes and refilled the *mochila* pouch, setting the real Consolidated Ophir dispatch aside to be sent next week. The whole process had taken less than an hour.

Fargo took the *mochila* and started out the door.

"You're going to ride it to Mud Springs, Skye?"

"See anybody else to do it?"

She stomped her foot. "There's no mirror here, or I would."

"You mean you want to ride forty miles through the night, then turn around?"

"Why not? I'm much lighter than you, so I can make good time. I may not be as good a rider, but I'd love to be able to write that I was the first and perhaps only lady rider in the history of the Pony Express. I'd have a firsthand account."

"Can you shoot?" Fargo wondered aloud.

"Most riders don't carry guns. They rely on speed to get away from trouble."

"You're sure?"

Jennifer nodded and started changing out of Mary's baggy dress into some of Arkins' clothes. Fargo felt like stopping her midway and hauling her off to bed. But this really was a choice between her going and him going, and if she wanted to make the run, well, he could use a good night's sleep. With her hair tucked under her hat, she could pass for a rider, especially in the dark.

It was Cody's grumbling that roused Fargo from a deep sleep. He was alternately mad and curious, and Fargo skirted most of his questions. The less anyone knew about this, the happier everyone would be. His disposition—and Fargo's—improved about an hour after sunrise, when Jennifer rode back in. Fargo sorted through the local dispatches and found nothing for Scott's Bluff. Moments later, Cody was on his way west, his head pounding as hard as his fresh horse.

"So how was it to be a Pony Express rider?"

Jennifer giggled. "That much time in the saddle made me sore. Maybe you could rub some of my aches in bed, Skye."

It was a pleasant fortnight before Ficklin arrived with a replacement agent and cook. That same day, Jennifer received a dispatch from New York, along with another copy of the *Herald*. She tore open the envelope and read hurriedly, while Fargo read the newspaper.

Jennifer's accounts of the Pony Express had been spread across the top of the front page of other editions, but bigger news had now displaced her writing.

Wall Street was agog because Josiah Abernathy's financial empire had collapsed. The story dryly explained that Abernathy had committed himself to the selling short of more Consolidated Ophir stock than actually existed. The ruined financier had been found dead in the study of his Fifth Avenue mansion. Police believed it was a suicide, although the investigation was continuing, because Abernathy had so many enemies.

Jennifer interrupted his reading. "Skye, Mr. Bennett wants to hire me full-time. He even has an assignment. According to the word that reached New York, there was an attempted raid at Rock Creek Station. The stable man, somebody named Jim Hickok, killed all the raiders. The *Herald* wants to know if I can interview him and send a full account."

Fargo groaned. "Hickok is just a fool hothead."

Jennifer smiled. "Well, I won't write about him that way. I can make Jim Hickok into a hero."

Fargo refilled his coffee while she scanned the newspaper and began to smile.

"You know, no one would ever believe the truth about how Abernathy fell," Jennifer mused. "He got crosswise of one man two thousand miles away, a man that didn't own much more than a horse and a few weapons." She started talking in the heroic way that her newspaper stories read.

"Wait a minute, Jennifer. The deal was that you'd keep me and my name out of what you wrote."

She batted her eyes teasingly. "Oh, all right, Skye. But only if you'll ride with me to Fort Kearney and explain some more about the country and the trail to me." She giggled. "When we're not in your bedroll, that is."

LOOKING FORWARD!
The following is the opening
section from the next novel in the exciting
Trailsman **series from Signet:**

THE TRAILSMAN #95
CRY REVENGE

1860, the Montana Territory
south of Crazy Peak, a land of
untamed beauty and untamed hate . . .

"You killed him. You stupid, stupid bastards. You killed the Trailsman," the woman screamed.

"You paid us to stop him and bring him to you," the man said, a rangy figure with a jagged scar on one cheek. The three men behind him nodded in agreement.

"Stopped doesn't mean killed, except to idiots like you," the woman flung back, her hands twisting together.

"He wouldn't stop. He kept riding. We had to shoot him," the scar-cheeked man insisted.

"You had to shoot him? My God, my God, what morons. You mean that's all you could think of doing," the woman said with scathing anger. She stepped out onto the porch to stare at the figure draped across the saddle of the magnificent, gleaming Ovaro, and a groan escaped her. "That's him," she said.

"I thought you never saw him before," one of the men said from the doorway.

"I never did, but that Ovaro of his was described to me as one of a kind. It sure is. So that's him, the Trailsman, dead." The woman returned to the house, her broad-cheeked, attractive face drawn. "God knows who all will come looking for him. He's not some drifter nobody's going to ask about. What if they come asking here?"

"You said stop him and bring him to you. That's what we did," the scar-cheeked man said with truculent persistence.

"I never said kill him. Never," the woman shouted, and with an effort, she gained control of herself, contempt flooding her face. "It's my fault for hiring stupid, trigger-happy louts like you," she said. "Bury him, but not near here. Then go to town. I'll get back to you."

"You better. You still owe us half the money you promised," the tall one said.

"Get out of here, Braden. Take the others with you. I've got to think about this," the woman said, and she followed the four men outside. "Put the Ovaro in the barn. I want him out of sight." She watched as her orders were obeyed and the four men rode off with their lifeless burden before returning to the house.

Once inside, she sank down on a sofa in the living room and put her hands to her face. "My God, my God, it all went wrong," she half-sobbed. "God, I wish I could take it all back, now." She sat, quietly sobbing, her face buried in her hands, bitterly aware that there was no changing what had been done, no turning back clocks, and her sobs of guilt filled the quiet room.

It had all begun in the warm, sunlit morning, a strange confluence of events that, as it so often happened in this land of wild, untamed beauty, turned calmness into violent tragedy. The big man with the lake-blue eyes had just finished a leisurely breakfast of johnnycakes and wild pears, and he was relaxing in the small arbor where he'd spent the night. The low Montana hills were green and ripe in the late summer's fullness, thick with staghorn sumac, hackberry, and black oak, all a banquet for the white-tailed deer and moose. He had just finished saddling the magnificently distinctive horse with its shining, pure-white midsection and glistening black fore and hindquarters, when he heard the sound from just beyond the curve in the narrow path. A man's voice, he frowned, pleading in it.

"I know, old girl, but keep trying . . . a little longer. Jesus, I'm sorry . . . I'm sorry," the voice said.

The big man stepped into the narrow path and saw the horse and rider come around the curve, the horse limping badly on its right foreleg. The rider saw him, halted, and jumped to the ground, a brawny man in his early thirties with a pleasant face and short-cropped hair. "Jeez, mister, am I glad to see you," he said.

"Name's Fargo, Skye Fargo," the big man said.

"John Wilson. I live about two miles up the road. It looks as though Annie, that's my wife, is gettin' ready to have her baby. I'm riding to Ashford to get Doc Ennis, but old Molly suddenly went lame on me," the man said.

Fargo knelt down beside the old mare's gray whiskers, his eyes scanning the right foreleg the horse gingerly held only barely touching the ground. He ran his hand over the mare's fetlock, up along the cannon bone and tendon, carefully felt her knee and finally drew his hand back.

"Can't feel any swelling," Fargo said. "Of course, that doesn't always mean much. Sometimes it takes a while for a sprain to swell up to where you can see it."

"I looked and couldn't see anything, either, but she's limping real bad. I don't think she can go another fifty yards," John Wilson said. "But I've got to get Doc Ennis for Annie. She's been having a hard time all along. Can I use your horse, mister? I know it's asking a lot, but Ashford's an hour from here."

"I know. I was there last night. Spent too much time with a bourbon bottle at the saloon," Fargo said with a touch of rue.

"I'll have your horse back before the morning's out," Wilson said. "But I'm real afraid for Annie if I don't get Doc Ennis to her."

"Wouldn't do this ordinarily, but this is the kind of time that calls for special things. Take him. Get the doc to your wife and that baby," Fargo said.

The man spun, pulled himself onto the Ovaro. "I'm real beholden to you, Fargo," he said. "The baby comes out fine we'll name him Fargo Wilson."

"Get riding, friend." Fargo smiled, and Wilson waved back as he raced off on the Ovaro.

Fargo stepped back into the little arbor and sat down against the trunk of a black oak. He let the warm feeling of a good deed curl inside him. Someone waited for him and he had still a distance to get there, but a new life was ready to come into being and the world could wait for that. Besides, last night's bourbon still affected him, and he welcomed another few hours' rest. He closed his eyes, listened to the sound of the bullock's orioles and the meadowlarks, and dozed in the warm sun.

When he finally snapped awake, he saw that the sun had passed to the other side of the hill. He pushed to his feet, a furrow digging into his brow. John Wilson should have been back with the doctor. He stepped into the path, peered downhill, but neither saw nor heard anything. The old mare stood quietly by, still favoring her right foreleg.

Fargo let another fifteen minutes pass. When Wilson still didn't appear, he felt the apprehension growing inside him. He walked to the mare, ran his hand down her foreleg again. There was still no sign of a swelling, so he picked up her foot, blacksmith-fashion, and ran his finger over the hoof. The shoe was on tight, he saw, and he again carefully ran his finger over the hoof, paused, felt again, and reached down to his calf. He drew the thin, double-bladed throwing knife from its calf holster and used the point to gently probe along the inner edge of the shoe, then halted. He worked the blade carefully until he pried loose a small, sharp stone that had lodged in the tender frog of the hoof.

He let the mare's foot down, trotted her in a circle, and she moved without the hint of a limp. He swung onto her broad back and headed down the path.

"Let's go, Molly," he muttered, his eyes on the ground. The Ovaro's tracks were easy to follow, the long, even stride unique, the hoofprints almost precisionlike in relation to each other, so unlike that of most horses. He'd ridden perhaps a half-hour, the frown deepening on his brow as he peered ahead and kept expecting to meet John Wilson and the doctor coming up the trail. But neither appeared, and his eyes continued to sweep the ground as he rode until suddenly he reined to a halt.

The Ovaro's tracks had suddenly changed, and he read the trail marks as other men read a book. The Ovaro had come to a stop and he saw the hoofprints of other horses. Four, he counted. The Ovaro had half-turned, then leapt forward, prints suddenly dug deeper into the ground. But the horse had come to a stop again, not more than a dozen feet on, and Fargo slid from the old mare to move forward on foot.

A thin layer of bunchgrass covered the ground, and he stared at an irregular imprint still clear where a body had hit the ground hard and lay still. Footprints edged the flat imprint. The riders of the other horses had dismounted. He noticed two sets of prints leave the Ovaro and return to the other horses. The tracks moved on again, the Ovaro's hoofprints moving with those of the other horses.

Fargo climbed onto the old mare again and followed. The hoofprints left the path and turned east, cutting along a wide swath between rows of hackberry, then moved downward with the land. The trees grew thicker, the road narrowing, and then he saw open land just beyond the treeline and a house a hundred yards on. He also saw the four horses and the Ovaro tethered outside the house, John Wilson's body on its back. The apprehension inside him had become a cold, grim knot in his stomach. The house faced open land, but trees and thick shrub grew almost to the very back of the house, and he sent the old mare in a circle through the trees until he was facing the rear of the house. He dismounted and moved forward on foot to the rear of the house, where a window hung open.

He lifted one long leg over the sill, pulled the other in after it, and straightened up inside a back room with a cot to one side and a small dresser nearby. He could hear the voices from the front of the house and he moved to where he could see down a short corridor into a larger room, where a woman paced up and down before four men.

Fargo watched her move back and forth, her voice coloring with anger, shock, helplessness, and he listened with astonishment spiraling. The woman was tall, in her early thirties, he guessed when he caught a glimpse of her face—dark-brown hair, a little heavy-featured, yet attractive enough, with wide cheekbones and full lips. At one point she stepped outside for a moment to quickly return, and he stayed motionless, listening to every word said.

When the four men finally rode away and the woman returned to the living room, Fargo listened to her sobbing for a few moments and then silently lifted himself through the window. Outside he dropped to one knee, his lips pulled back in a grimace laced with its own bitterness. Fate had struck with a terrible twist of tragic irony, events conspiring to make a mockery of the lives of good men and the actions of scoundrels. He felt the awe inside himself as he paused to digest what had happened.

Four gunslingers had tried to kill him with callous impunity—and thought they had done so. The woman had set it all in motion to find it shattering in her face, actions exploding beyond her wishes and her control. An innocent man lay dead and, despite the twists of fate, his blood stained her hands. And somehow, someway, he was a part of it. Fargo frowned.

The four cold-blooded killers would have to pay. The woman had searing questions to answer, and he had explanations to uncover. But there was something else. A new life might never reach the world, an innocent man's heritage ended before it could begin. Everything paled before that. Everything else could wait.

Bitter with anger, Fargo rose and strode into the trees. He retrieved the old mare and circled behind the house again to where the barn stood some twenty-five yards beyond the house. He moved to the rear of the barn, saw a back door, and left the mare in the trees. With a quick, darting stride, he moved into the open and ran into the barn. Two heifers occupied a box stall and he quickly spied the Ovaro tied to the beam at the back of the barn. He untied the horse, slowly and quietly opened the rear door of the barn, and led the horse into the trees. He climbed into the saddle, took the mare's reins in one hand, and stayed in the tree cover as he moved away from the house.

When he was far enough away, he left the trees, returned to the narrow trail, and put the Ovaro into a canter. The sun had moved into the midday sky when he reached Ashford, asked directions, and was directed to the doctor's house at the edge of town.

The man answered the door, rimless glasses on a mild face, a checked vest over a white shirt. "It's Annie Wilson. She's in trouble," Fargo said, and the man's mild face took on instant concern.

"I'll get my horse," he said, and disappeared into the house. He emerged moments later along a side alley, and Fargo swung in beside him. "Where's John? With Annie?" Doc Ennis asked.

Fargo drew a deep breath. "You're going to have trouble believing this," Fargo said. "But every terrible, rotten word of it is true." He spoke in terse sentences as they rode into the hills, and when he finished, the man's face wore shock and pain. It took the doctor minutes before he found words, and his voice was almost a whisper.

"The baby. I must save the baby," he said, and sent his horse into a gallop.

The small house, hand-built, with a stable behind, came into view as the sun began to slide toward the horizon, and as Fargo halted and swung to the ground, he heard the woman's moaning cries.

Doc Ennis was already at the door and turned to him

as he entered. "Hot water and towels, Fargo," the doctor said. "Quick."

A low fire burned in the hearth. Fargo added wood and swung a big black kettle of water over the flame. He found towels in a cabinet and followed the doctor's instructions as the woman's screams grew louder, wilder.

Doc Ennis worked with her, perspired as the hours passed and the night descended. But he was patient, careful, in what was plainly a very difficult labor.

Annie Wilson asked for her husband, and Doc Ennis gave her reasons why he had not returned, each one enough to satisfy. Finally, after the night had grown long, the woman's time came.

Fargo watched and felt helpless, but the miracle that was life went on and finally he heard the new sound, the cry of a new life, surprisingly strong and lusty. He went outside and leaned against the side of the house.

John Wilson would live. Birth was more than a beginning. It was a bridge made of flesh and bone and spirit, where yesterday crossed into tomorrow. But he felt his fists clench. None of the wonderfulness of it could change the terrible tragedy that had occurred. Nothing could make up for that. But the four killers would still pay. Then there were questions to be answered, Fargo promised himself.

He turned as Doc Ennis came from the house and sank down wearily on a rock. "She had a hard time. She'll need care and rest," he said. "I'm not telling her about John until she's stronger. I've given her enough excuses to satisfy."

"Somebody's going to have to stay with her," Fargo said.

"I'll take her and the baby back to my place tomorrow," Doc Ennis said. "Could you stay long enough to help?"

"Be my pleasure," Fargo said.

"The Wilsons have a road cart behind the house. We'll hitch the old mare to it. I'll drive and Annie can hold the baby. I'd feel better if someone else was with us," the doctor said.

"Count on it." Fargo nodded. "I'll take care of bringing your horse back."

The doctor rose, his face drawn. "I'm going in and sleep some," he said. "See you in the morning."

Fargo rose and took his bedroll down, rolled it out at the edge of the small cleared section of land, and went to sleep knowing he'd never know what made the world turn as it did or why the just suffered so much injustice. But then he wasn't alone in wondering that, he knew, though it was small comfort.

The night stayed quiet and he woke only at the cries of the baby, which were quickly satisfied. The morning sun came and he let another hour go by before he rose, washed at the small well he found, and dressed.

The house was quiet and Doc Ennis didn't appear till almost noon. "She had a good night," he said. "But I'd like to let her rest most of the day before we take to traveling."

"Whatever you think best," Fargo said. "I'll be here whenever you're ready to move."

The man nodded and returned to the house.

Fargo saddled the Ovaro and leisurely rode higher into the hills. He halted where the path leveled off and let him look down at the land below and beyond. Land of the mountains, the Spanish explorers had named it, *Montana*, the territory embracing the Bitterroot Range of the great Rockies that stretched from north to south. In the vast, ripe terrain, a storehouse for every kind of game, bird, and fish, the redman had carved out his own domains. The Arapaho rode the lush land, as did the Assiniboin, the Gros Ventre, and the Cheyenne. But mostly, this was the land of the Sioux, who crossed its richness from border to border, warriors as much at home on the plains as in the mountains. And now the white man invaded, pressed tentative tentacles of his own civilization on the land. At a terrible price, though, in human lives, a price extracted not only by the Indian but by nature as well, for despite its rich gifts, the Montana land demanded strength and endurance from those who would live on it.

Fargo's eyes moved slowly across the undulating hills, drifted to the great peaks beyond where the Bitterroot Range and the Salmon River Mountains rose to almost touch the sky. Bringing his gaze back closer, he picked out passages below, marked them in his mind to use when he continued on north. The letter of agreement in his jacket pocket reminded him that he was expected within the week, and he turned the Ovaro around and moved back down the hill to the house.

Doc Ennis waited outside as the afternoon sun moved across the sky. Fargo saw the road cart hitched and waiting.

"I'll get Annie up. It'll be night before we reach Ashford," the doctor said. "We'll be traveling real slow."

"I expect so." Fargo had the reins of the doctor's horse in hand when the man led the woman from the house. She carried the small bundle swathed in a blanket, and Doc Ennis helped her into the cart. Fargo glimpsed a woman younger than he'd expected, hair pulled up atop her head but still with long, straggly ends. Her eyes met his and she managed a small smile as he nodded.

Doc Ennis took the reins and Fargo sent the pinto on ahead, pulled the mare behind him. He held to a walk as Doc Ennis moved the light road cart as slowly and carefully as he could over the uneven ground, and the night descended long before they reached the town. But finally, they arrived at Ashford and the doctor's small house, where he quickly took the woman and baby inside. He returned in minutes to take the reins of his horse.

"Annie Wilson thanks you and I thank you, Fargo," the man said. "What happens now?"

"When the time comes, you can tell her the men who gunned down her husband have paid for it," Fargo said.

"Maybe I'd best wait till afterward, when it's a sure thing," the doctor said.

"It's a sure thing," Fargo said.

Ennis studied his face for a long moment. "I guess it is," the man said. "Good luck, Fargo." He turned, led the mare away, and Fargo's lake-blue eyes had become the frigid blue of an ice floe. He led the Ovaro by the cheek strap as he slowly walked down the wide street of Ashford. The four men he sought would be only one place in any town, the saloon. He'd give them a chance to talk, but he knew the type. They'd answer with their six-guns. Perhaps that was just as well, he grunted grimly.

The woman would be next, he vowed. She held the real answers. He reached the double doors of the saloon, pushed them open, and stepped into the smoke-filled haze of the room.